6¢p

'Let me protect you.'

Lauren couldn't hide her mistrust. Ryan had told her to take her freedom while she might and here he was, hours later, inviting her back into captivity.

'If you're innocent it would provide a perfect solution. Some men have no respect for beauty, Lauren. In fact some men don't respect anything at all. You'll be safe with me...'

Dear Reader

Easter is upon us, and with it our thoughts turn to the meaning of Easter. For many, it's a time when Nature gives birth to all things, so what better way to begin a new season of love and romance than by reading some of the new authors whom we have recently introduced to our lists? Watch out for Helen Brooks, Jenny Cartwright, Liz Fielding, Sharon Kendrick and Catherine O'Connor—all of whom have books coming out this spring!

The Editor

Christine Greig works full-time as a senior marketing manager in the communications industry. This involves a great deal of travel, both within Europe and the United States, which she enjoys very much. She has a BA Hons degree and a diploma in marketing. She is in her thirties, came originally from North Yorkshire, England, and is married.

Recent titles by the same author:

STRONG MAGIC

EDGE OF WILDNESS

BY

CHRISTINE GREIG

MILLS & BOON LIMITED
ETON HOUSE   18-24 PARADISE ROAD
RICHMOND   SURREY   TW9 1SR

*First published in Great Britain 1993
by Mills & Boon Limited*

© Christine Greig 1993

*Australian copyright 1993
Philippine copyright 1993
This edition 1993*

ISBN 0 263 77970 X

*Set in Times Roman 10 on 11½ pt.
01-9304-55703 C*

Made and printed in Great Britain

CHAPTER ONE

'BREATHE heat, Lauren,' the photographer called out to the willowy model, who was supposed to be in charge of a state-of-the-art tractor, of all things, being given the glamour treatment for a sales push. This particular piece of farm machinery sold itself. Farmers weren't thought so gullible that a pretty girl and a glossy magazine cover would make them part with their hard-earned money, but to have efficiency and style was a winning combination. Daniels and Blackthorn apparently thought so—they were paying the bills.

Lauren Walsh maintained an uncomfortable pose, her eyes drawing the camera to her as if it were remote-controlled. She thought of hot earth, the smell of corn, endless blue skies, and was quite involved in her own private fantasy when the camera stopped whirring and the crew relaxed.

'Nice one, Lauren,' Jacko Bryan saluted, looking pleased with himself. 'I think that wraps it up.'

Lauren blinked then focused rapidly on a man in a navy pin-striped suit who was leaning against one of the monster machines not being used in the final sequence of photographs. He had been watching her—not an unusual occurrence in her line of work—but he didn't drop his gaze when she found him out, and that unnerved her.

'Checking out we weren't wasting film?' Jacko Bryan joked, confirming that the man was an executive of the firm commissioning the advertising. 'Checking out something, anyway.' He grinned over his shoulder at

Lauren, who didn't appreciate the male camaraderie that placed her in the category of 'woman'—to be discussed and not introduced.

'Looking for this?' The man held out her holdall, inviting her nearer.

Eyes glittering like green fires, Lauren tossed back her mane of dark hair and approached, only to have the bag withdrawn and a strong, masculine hand extended in what she felt was a false gesture of friendship.

'Ryan Daniels,' he introduced himself, his fingers closing around Lauren's, his grasp firm. 'I apologise for thinking getting your picture taken was easy money. Watching you just then, I could almost smell the corn.'

Her eyes were riveted on his, aware that he thought her profession frivolous and 'corn' had more than one meaning. What she saw there made her heart beat wildly. Here was a man used to taking what he wanted and, she intuitively guessed, despised the ease of conquest.

From what she had gleaned from the other models' chatter Ryan Daniels came from an immensely wealthy family and was carving his own legend in the business world. He reaped all the benefits wealth and power could accrue and that included the pick of society's beauties. Lauren guessed he wouldn't be short of female company if he were penniless—he had a brand of dynamic good looks that would guarantee success. His hair was the colour of old gold, cut short and swept back from his forehead to reveal a lean, angular face. His eyes were hooded blue-grey, set above a straight nose and firm, very masculine mouth.

'Lauren Walsh.' Her voice sounded husky to her own ears. Something about him made her feel as if she was flirting with danger, and she didn't like that; she liked to feel safe.

'Walsh?' He repeated her surname with a slight questioning inflexion, his eyes compelling, his fingers letting go slowly of hers. 'I have an employee of that name. Any connection?'

'My brother.' Lauren felt as if she'd been holding her breath for a long time, and took a gulp of air, her breasts lifting as her lungs expanded.

He noted the movement and the curling of her hands into fists. Ryan Daniels's mouth turned upwards into a smile, the spell of some barely exercised charisma keeping Lauren rooted to the spot.

'Yours?'

A surge of embarrassment scalded her face in colour when she realised he was holding out the holdall once more. Snatching at it, she was halted as he didn't immediately let go.

'Are you free for dinner this evening? If this campaign is successful, I may have some more work for you. We could discuss a project I have in mind,' he suggested.

'I'm busy.' She exercised the minimum of politeness, amazed at the audacity of the man.

'Cancel whatever or whoever it is. I'll give you a far better time.' He brushed her jaw with the back of his knuckles in mock punishment for her resistance.

'I have an appointment with a good book and a cup of cocoa. I'm afraid I can't be tempted.' She tugged her bag free. He had pushed her into being rude and her emerald eyes burned with inner rage at the derisive arch of his eyebrow.

'I clearly can't compete.' His gaze moved past her to where Jacko and his crew were packing their equipment away. 'It's the first time I've met a model who can't handle a pass.'

Lauren would have loved to part on a witty line that would have cut him dead but she merely gave him an incensed look, his soft laughter making her spine stiffen as she moved past him and made for the changing-rooms.

Lauren changed out of the country gear she had worn for the session, dressing for the bleak February day waiting for her outside. The oversized hand-knitted jumper she pulled on swamped her slender frame and with black stirrup leggings and ankle boots she felt warm enough to survive the journey to the car.

'Oh, the briefcase.' She frowned, glancing around. It was under the pile of discarded clothes. Unearthing it, she hung up her outfit, noticing that none of the others had bothered.

Before leaving, she automatically checked the mirror— not out of personal vanity, but the agency boss, Melanie Peters, was a stickler for keeping the fantasy image of her models going even when the shoot was finished.

Lauren's dark hair pooled over her shoulders, her make-up hardly noticeable to go with the 'country girl' image. A lingering confusion darkened the green eyes seriously returning her inspection. She hadn't handled Ryan Daniels very well; it had hardly been professional to go on the attack like that. Some of her colleagues could refuse a man and leave him feeling flattered; why had she reacted so defensively? Probably because she had been caught staring like a schoolgirl, she was scrupulously honest with herself. It was a novelty for her to find a man attractive, even if his personality made him totally abhorrent to her.

Dismissing Ryan Daniels from her thoughts, Lauren found that the satisfaction of a fatter bank balance awaiting her weekend purchases cheered her immensely. Money was important to Lauren. It symbolised safety. Many of her friends from the London College of Fashion had chosen to work on their designs while they were un-employed. She couldn't do that. She needed to feel she could move on if things went badly, pay for four walls of her own. It was silly really; she was an adult now—the fears from the past should fade. But at twenty-three she still hadn't resolved the conflicts of her adolescence and a pay-cheque still had the power to chase back those dark fears.

She walked to the lift, her mind idly dwelling on the image of heat and the gold rustle of crops in the fields conjured up for the camera. An English winter was long and tedious enough to make summer seem like a fairy-tale...

Gone were the imaginary corn fields of some vast prairie and in its place an angry security guard was taking possession of her brother's briefcase.

'Will you please come this way, miss?' the uniformed man pompously requested. 'It's a routine security check.'

Shrugging, she followed him into an office which had TV monitors covering one wall. Hands on hips, she watched with mounting horror as the briefcase was opened and the man took out a file, viewing it significantly.

'What's going on?' she demanded, horribly confused. The man turned away, talking into a radio transmitter he had clipped to his jacket. The words 'suspect apprehended' made her eyes widen in protest.

'It's called industrial espionage,' the security man sneered at what he was sure was feigned innocence. 'What you have in that briefcase——'

'But...' Lauren's distressed explanation faltered as Ryan Daniels entered the room, his glance assessing as he took in the situation.

'What have you got, Davis?' He accepted the file, perusing its contents, his eyes flicking upwards to view Lauren's bewilderment. 'I want the spot-checks kept up. See to it, will you?'

Sitting on the edge of the desk near her, he nudged the folder towards her, his expression demanding. 'Explain.' The command was short and sharp but effective.

Lauren swallowed and took a deep breath. 'I—I don't know if I can.' Seeing dissatisfaction mark his features, she stumbled into speech. 'My brother asked me to bring his briefcase home; he'd forgotten it—but Derek would never pinch anything. He wouldn't,' she insisted. 'I know he wouldn't.'

It was all so simple! Her brother, Derek, had asked her to pick up his briefcase from the building. It was a coincidence for them to work for the same firm. Derek had been working for the Daniels Corporation for two years as a designer for their industrial hardware. She didn't know what was in the briefcase but Derek, she knew, would never be involved in anything suspect.

'Where is your brother?' Ryan Daniels's cool voice commanded attention.

'I don't know.' She bit her lip, finding little warmth in the pale eyes regarding her. 'I mean...' She swallowed. It sounded so bad. But the usually elementally responsible Derek had gone away for a weekend that was shrouded in secrecy. She was sure they were both victims of someone's attempt to smuggle out valuable secrets, but on the face of things it looked very black.

'Do you know where he is or not?' The voice penetrated her confusion.

'No, I...' She took a deep breath, her green eyes tangling with the rapier-like gaze shrewdly assessing her disturbed state. 'He said he was going away for the weekend and he'd forgotten his briefcase. Derek's not a thief! Someone must have put those papers in his case.'

The slight twist of Ryan Daniels's mouth spoke volumes. The security guard gave a sneering laugh.

'And I'm Mary Poppins.'

'All right, Davis. That's enough. Can you organise some tea for Miss Walsh? She looks as if she might faint,' Ryan said.

Lauren was bewildered. Nothing about him suggested he sympathised with her in the least. She watched him move to the window as the security man left. Separating the blinds, he looked out into the cold winter's night. She was left to watch and wait. It was a form of refined torture. He looked as if he'd forgotten her existence but something about him made her doubt she'd make the door.

She studied her adversary, for such she classed him. He was no less determined than the security man Davis; he just used different techniques.

'I suppose you might get a suspended sentence.' His gaze had returned to her and the blinds fell back with a clatter, making her jump. 'Though I doubt modelling will provide a lucrative career for you in the future.'

This time his eyes assessed her as a woman and some small spark of indignation in Lauren grew.

'This is ridiculous! Nothing has been stolen. You have whatever was in the...' Mocking grey eyes watched her mind grope towards cognition.

'It's not the first time, Lauren. Security has been tightened in response to minor breaches over the last three months. The material you attempted to liberate was, no doubt, the pay-off.' His eyes were insolent. 'I thought I'd paid you well enough for draping yourself over our new tractor range but apparently you aspire to greater things.'

'If this is your idea of a practical joke,' she hurried into indignant speech, 'it's in very bad taste. Just because I refused to go out with you doesn't give you any right to frighten me like this.'

Ryan Daniels let his eyes wander over her face, his gaze resting on her mouth with a moment's indolence that was broken by the reappearance of the security guard.

'I assure you this is no practical joke, Lauren.'

He meant it, she could tell, and an icy finger of fear stroked down her spine.

'I brought a cup for you, Mr Daniels, just in case you wanted some,' Davis said.

'Thank you.' Ryan handed Lauren hers, observing the cup rattle against the saucer as her hand shook. 'Drink it,' he instructed, 'you look as if you need it.'

Lauren felt the tea scald her mouth and go down the wrong way. A paroxysm of coughs shook her slender frame. Ryan Daniels approached her and removed the cup and saucer from her hand, directing a series of smart slaps to her back. Tears mingled with the effects of a choking fit and she looked as waif-like as her portfolio suggested.

A crisp white handkerchief was given in a perfunctory manner and both men stood regarding their catch with the uncomfortable air of men confronted with a weeping woman.

'I'm sorry...' She wiped her eyes, taking a deep breath. 'I feel as if I've walked into a n-nightmare.'

Ryan Daniels felt his much vaunted shrewdness with regard to judging character under severe threat. Everything told him that this girl was the icing on the cake of a major security breach. If he hadn't insisted on random spot-checks his security team would have been offering to carry the briefcase for her. She was certainly something to look at.

Ryan indulged himself in a lengthy inspection. Her rich brown hair had chestnut lights glinting in the rippling darkness. Fine brows arched over green eyes with dark, secretive lashes. He'd seen some of the publicity work. Lauren Walsh's face seduced the camera with its heart-shaped perfection. That trembling mouth could pout delightfully... He snapped back to attention as the woman caught his regard and something in the tear-stained depths reproved him.

Frowning, he bit his lip thoughtfully, his hands pushing into the pockets of his trousers, the navy pin-striped suit he wore adjusting itself to his movements, the inner midnight-blue silk proclaiming an excellent tailor. Various arguments presented their case and he assessed them with lightning speed.

'You can go.' He nodded to the offending briefcase. 'I'll need that for fingerprints. Davis, get something similar to replace it and put back the non-contentious articles it contained.'

'But Mr——'

'Miss Walsh is clearly not involved.' He let his eyes slide over her, noticing the surprise, gratitude and puzzlement chasing across her features. 'I want nothing more said about this incident, Davis, understood? Just you and I know about it. Let's leave it at that.'

'Yes, sir.' The security guard looked put out but squashed his protests. 'I'll fetch another briefcase.'

Lauren was confused. One minute Ryan Daniels had been talking about a suspended prison sentence and the next he was letting her go. She tried to express her thanks but saw that he was watching her again in the same way as he had when she had been on the modelling assignment.

'Hasn't anyone ever told you it's rude to stare?' She found herself flung back into conflict.

'It isn't exactly polite to pinch industrial secrets,' he reminded her. 'One way or another I'm going to capture you, Lauren Walsh, and when I do you won't get away. So take your freedom while you can.'

Lauren left the environs of Daniels and Blackthorn as if the devil were at her heels. She didn't question the provision of the new briefcase; she was too distressed for it to seem odd that Ryan Daniels should replace it. She flung it into the boot of her car with her holdall and then scrambled into the scarlet Mini with more speed than elegance.

Her mission was to find Derek and make some sense of what had happened. Despite this necessity her mind kept playing back Ryan Daniels's words. Capture, he had said, capture, not catch. An omen of foreboding told her that Ryan Daniels intended her for no prison but a cage of his own making!

Returning to the flat she shared with her brother in Catford, Lauren moved over to Derek's bureau as soon as her key allowed her access and rummaged through it until she found his address book.

The next few hours were laboriously spent ringing up his friends; some she knew and many she didn't, but no one seemed to have a clue where Derek was. One of the numbers with no name and address next to it was answered by a voice that was stiffly formal and requested whom she was calling. She didn't know, but asked if he knew a Derek Walsh. The advice that she had almost certainly got the wrong number was contradicted when she repeated it back to the man on the other end of the line.

'This is the Daniels household,' the stiff voice informed her. 'The number is ex-directory. Would you like to speak to Mr Daniels if he's available?'

'No—oh, no!' She felt her breath rush from her lungs as if she had been punched. 'Thank you.' She hastily put down the phone as if it contained a devil.

Where was Derek? It wasn't like him just to disappear into the blue. They were the only close family each other possessed and they were very close. From what he had let slip she had received the impression that the weekend away had been a snap decision. Lauren had suspected her strait-laced brother had become romantically entangled. She had intended to tease the details out of him when they next met. Such light-heartedness seemed a million miles away that cold Friday night in London.

Darkness fell as she continued to plod her way through the remainder of the address book. The usual feeling of warmth and security her home conjured up evaded her that night. She tried to reassure herself by darting little glances at the huge couch with its cream covers, the thin brown lines criss-crossing in a generous check. It was festooned with cushions she had collected on her travels, some ornately decorated, others plump velvet. The carpet was a pale beige and unobtrusive. A bookcase took up one alcove, its mahogany wood gleaming richly, the glass-fronted doors shining and lovingly polished. A great gilt mirror took up pride of place above the fire. It looked as if it should be in a star's dressing-room or in some exotic boudoir. Derek hadn't been sure of that but Lauren insisted it added an aspect of fun to the room, along with the audacious cream and blue flowered curtains. If her brother had his way, they would have lived in something resembling the public library.

She looked at the mirror, hoping it would bring a smile to her lips, but everything in the room seemed to lack the security she sought. They were all transitory props, easily moved on, easily forgotten. This haven had been lovingly constructed, but Ryan Daniels loomed over the safety of this small corner of London and made it all look fragile and perilous. Dark fear struck into her heart. Lauren had been frightened before. Frightened at a time a teenager was most vulnerable. Then Derek had rescued her and had made her world safe again. It was her turn to do the same thing for him. The fear that she wasn't strong enough to stand up to a character like Ryan Daniels made her frenetic progress through his address book unrelenting.

Two hours later she dozed off and slept until the phone ringing woke her. She grabbed at the receiver and blinked as the line went dead. Getting up, she moved to close the curtains and froze as she saw two men trying to get into her car.

Scrambling back to the phone, she rang the police on the emergency number and then checked that the door was locked. Her new Mini was her pride and joy and she sat huddled on the couch in a trembling rage. Common sense told her to stay where she was but she felt like opening the window and pelting the unknown burglars with every item that came to hand.

A dark, viperish suspicion twisted silently in her mind. The briefcase, Derek being missing and now the robbery worked into a mysterious triad. Lauren became panicked, deeply worried for her brother's safety.

By the time the police came, the two men trying to get into the car had gone. She checked the Mini over with one of the officers and found the briefcase and her holdall were missing. It had been a professional job, he told her; the boot was barely scratched. Not knowing how far to incriminate herself or her brother, she kept quiet about the incident earlier that day. She would inform Ryan Daniels of the theft and see what he made of it. After all, it proved her innocence. Why would anyone break into her car if she was in cahoots with the criminals bent on industrial espionage?

Ryan Daniels viewed his companion with a degree of disenchantment. Chantal Rabanne was exquisite but he was bored. He had made the date with Chantal after Lauren Walsh had refused him, but found, much to his surprise, that being in need of female company did not mean that any attractive woman would suffice.

He needed to marry or at least show signs of a lasting commitment. Watching Lauren Walsh that afternoon had given him an inkling how to satiate a powerful physical attraction and appease his father at the same time. Discovering that Lauren was either a thief or her brother's accomplice was a considerable fly in the ointment, but even with this handicap the idea of a relationship with her was more appealing than facing the inanities of social chatter over the breakfast table every morning.

A tide of frustration rose within him. Why was his father being so capricious? He had proved himself, expanding the corporation, already owning a substantial proportion of the shares. He was in direct line for the presidency and the emergence of Richard Harrington as a contender because the human oil slick had the enterprise to dazzle his sister, Penelope, was infuriating.

'You're very quiet, darling.' Chantal sounded disgruntled. 'Is something wrong?'

His name being paged allowed him to avoid false assurances. He stood up. 'Excuse me.'

Upon picking up the receiver of the phone indicated, he was surprised to find out that events had moved more quickly than he had imagined. Making apologies to Chantal, he offered to see her home but she sulkily refused, having spied friends at another table. With a feeling of relief Ryan was glad to seek the dark night air rather than spend another minute longer in the restaurant.

His chauffeur Mitch Harrison drove him to the Catford address.

'First floor, boss,' the man instructed, parking behind the Mini and awaiting instructions.

'Wait here.' Ryan Daniels got out of the car feeling incongruous in his dinner-jacket.

Lauren had been alerted by the sound of the Mercedes's engine and watched Ryan Daniels approach the building with mixed feelings. She hadn't expected him to call that night; it was nearly eleven o'clock, but the departure of the police had left her feeling distinctly vulnerable and her brother's employer was better company than none at all.

She opened the door as he reached the top of the flight of stairs, her eyes green seas of trouble as they suffered the rake of his.

'Exciting life you lead,' he greeted her, 'for someone addicted to novels and cocoa.'

'I didn't mean to drag you away from anything.' She shivered as he brought in the cold night air with him, finding his sarcasm dented any gratitude she might have felt for his swift attention.

'You didn't.' He viewed the apartment with interest. 'It's very "you",' he remarked, sitting on the arm of the couch, watching her intently. 'And?'

'Someone broke into my car.' She frowned, assuming the superior butler would have passed on the message. 'They stole the briefcase.'

'They?' He knew about the car and where the hapless thieves had taken the briefcase.

She nodded, expecting him to reach the same conclusion as she had. 'Derek hasn't come back home. Anyway, he wouldn't steal his own briefcase, would he?'

'So what are you saying? Derek's innocent? Did the police catch these thieves?'

'No, they'd gone but——'

'Your car doesn't look damaged. Am I expected to believe both yourself and your brother are innocent because of a few scratches on your boot?'

'The police have got the report——' she began.

'I'm sure. It might work for a small insurance fraud but it hardly clears either of you, does it?' He watched the protest grow in her eyes and waved it down in a bored fashion.

'Whether Derek's involved or not, there was nothing in the briefcase. No one but myself and Davis knows you were intercepted. Whichever way you look at it, whoever wants the contents of the briefcase thinks they're in your possession.' He watched her eyes widen with fear. 'If you're not involved you've got a problem.'

'But I don't know anything!' She bit her lip, her mind racing. 'What about the police?'

Ryan Daniels shrugged. 'As far as I'm concerned nothing has been stolen. Industrial espionage is not good for the share index. I deal with my own problems.'

'Well, bully for you!' Her anger exploded. 'What am I supposed to do? I don't know where my brother is. I know he's an innocent bystander in all this. He could be in trouble and all you can talk about is the share prices!'

Observing her anger, he pushed himself to his feet, approaching her, surveying the fine bone-structure of her face with an intensity that made her blush.

'I object to you——'

'You need my protection.' He reached out, taking a strand of her hair between finger and thumb, his eyes darkening when she pulled away and glared at him. 'You can't stay here. If the thieves breaking into your car were involved with the security breaches at Daniels and Blackthorn, they'll know by now that the briefcase was empty.'

Instinctively Lauren moved towards the phone. She might have some explaining to do to the police but she wasn't prepared to get any deeper into an intrigue she knew nothing about.

'That wouldn't be very smart.' Ryan leisurely intercepted her, his hand resting lightly over hers, keeping the receiver in place. 'The police like results. You were found in possession of material competitors would pay a great deal for.' He let her finish the equation. 'I have a much better suggestion.' His voice silked insidiously into her mind.

'You have?' Her doubts were legion when she met his smoky gaze, aware of the quiet triumph there.

'Let me protect you.'

Lauren couldn't hide her mistrust. He'd told her to take her freedom while she might, and here he was, hours later, inviting her back into captivity.

'If you're innocent it would provide a perfect solution. Some men have no respect for beauty, Lauren. In fact some men don't respect anything at all. You'll be safe with me. And I promise you first-hand information on your brother's whereabouts. Make no doubt about it, I will find him, and I would guess you'd like to be there when I do, to make sure he gets a fair deal.'

For endless moments Lauren was lost in his masculine strength, drawn, despite herself, to the powerful aura of the man. Her earlier impression of him as a dangerous enemy became hopelessly confused. The wall-lights made his hair gleam. The golden colour darkened towards his scalp, giving the impression of light and darkness. His eyes were also a deceptive blue-grey. It was as if any clear definition of Ryan Daniels were not to be had easily. Virile intelligence hid behind those hooded eyes, and it gave the lingering observation he subjected her to a potency that ensnared her.

'My family home is in Mayfair. We have plenty of spare rooms.' He allayed one of her fears and left her ridden by a host of others.

Lauren considered refusing his offer and going to a hotel instead, but then if any further incidents were to occur she wanted a cast-iron alibi. She also intended to make sure Derek was provided with a good solicitor when he came face to face with his employer.

Ryan took his hand off hers, sensing her weakening, surprised when she picked up the receiver and offered it to him.

'Don't you want to ring ahead and tell them to lock up the silver?' She fought free of the spell those light eyes cast over her.

'Any further thefts I'll take back in kind,' he replied.

'What does that mean?' She went to her bedroom door, preparing to pack a bag.

'Be a good girl and you won't find out.'

She froze in the doorway, her hair rippling in a dark tide over her shoulders. In dangerous waters, sharks were better friends than enemies, but this one was willing to gobble her up if she got too close.

'Who's going to protect me from you?' she asked frostily.

'Don't you trust yourself, Lauren?' he mocked gently. 'I like my women willing.'

'No danger, then,' she returned slickly, but didn't linger to hear his response.

CHAPTER TWO

LAUREN awoke the next morning in a strange room with a young girl dressed in a maid's outfit placing a tea-tray on the bedside table.

It all came back to her—the electronic gates closing smoothly behind the Mercedes as the shadowy outline of the Daniels mansion loomed as both sanctuary and a place of confinement. Even when bewildered and distressed, Lauren had noted the discreet cameras monitoring the drive.

'Mr Ryan would like you to join him for breakfast. Is there anything special you'd like?' the girl asked.

'What? Oh, just orange juice.' She glanced at the bedside clock and saw that it was seven o'clock. A model's life was one of intense activity interspersed with periods of resting. Lauren liked to breakfast at eight-thirty and take her time about it when she wasn't working.

'Does Mr Daniels always breakfast at this time?' she asked, more to confirm her impression of him as a workaholic than any criticism.

'He's usually at the office by now.' The girl sounded impressed. 'He works very hard.'

Lauren imagined he was one of those tireless executives who spent every working hour making deals. She had watched a documentary on corporate high-flyers and it made her feel tired.

After showering, she dressed in clothes she had hastily packed the night before. Matching a pair of high-waisted black wool trousers with a silk top and a short, tailored

22

cherry-red jacket, she felt armoured for the confrontation ahead.

'Good morning,' Ryan greeted her. His breakfast consisted of a cup of coffee.

She returned the greeting, not really knowing what was good about it and suspecting the day was about to get worse. Her fruit juice appeared and a fresh pot of expensive coffee was placed at Ryan's elbow.

Surveying him, she tried to guess what he was thinking. He was dressed more casually than the day before, which suggested a more relaxed mood. He wore cords with a crew-necked jersey in ecru and had a tan-coloured suede jacket luxuriating across the back of a spare chair.

'What had you planned for today? Had you anything lined up workwise?'

'It's Saturday.' Lauren had misplaced the day in the summons to breakfast. 'No, I——'

'What?'

'I usually do my shopping and give the flat a thorough clean,' she offered, feeling the domestic details of her life were a little mundane.

'I was thinking more along the lines of searching for your brother,' Ryan Daniels prompted drily.

Lauren frowned. 'But he's gone away for the weekend; I wouldn't know where to start——'

'Where does he usually spend his weekends? Has he any favourite haunts?'

'Yes, but——'

'Lauren, we have to consider that Derek might not have been strictly truthful.' Ryan Daniels's eyes glinted with impatience as if he suspected she was playing dumb. 'Don't you think it's strange that he didn't leave a phone number or a place for you to contact him?'

Lauren's confusion showed clearly on her face, her green eyes darkening dramatically. 'He's a fine man,' she maintained. 'I'm proud of him.'

Ryan's mouth firmed in exasperation, his gaze hard, the colour of polished steel. 'You're avoiding my question.'

'No, I'm not. You're trying to imply Derek is involved in some kind of subterfuge and I'm telling you he isn't.'

'Let's start again,' her interrogator grated. 'Where would your brother go in the city if he wanted to have a good time?'

Lauren sipped her fruit juice contemplatively. 'He likes museums,' she offered. 'Art galleries, that sort of thing.'

'What about friends—has he a girlfriend?' Ryan Daniels clearly didn't find Derek's cultural pastimes significant.

'I think so. That's where I thought he'd gone this weekend. But he's never mentioned anyone in particular and, before you ask, he didn't say where he was going.'

'No name, no place—no idea.' Ryan's tone showed what he thought of that. 'The noble Derek doesn't keep you in the picture, does he? Why? Are you the possessive type?'

'Not in the least.' She was hostile. She didn't like to admit that Derek's behaviour was out of character. Normally, he made sure she could contact him. 'Derek takes his responsibilities seriously. I can only think the weekend was planned hastily. He wouldn't tell me details because—well, he thinks he should set a good example . . .' She faltered under his withering gaze.

'Just because I can't quite bring myself to throw you into gaol doesn't mean I'll swallow any yarn you care to spin. You're over the age of consent. I can't believe you haven't had a string of lovers,' he said.

Lauren coloured delicately pink, her dark lashes shielding her expression. 'Bed-hopping isn't compulsory, Mr Daniels, whatever you may think.'

Searching her face, his expression was one of curiosity mingled with disbelief. 'There's no man in your life, then?' he pressed, annoyed for revealing his interest.

'No.' Her reply was simple and unembellished.

He laughed, self-derision evident, flinging himself back in his chair. 'So some small corner of Catford exists in a Victorian time-warp. You must take me for a fool.'

'I think you're a cynical man,' she returned quietly. 'And you know what they say about cynics...?'

'Remind me.' His voice made the small hairs on the back of her neck rise.

'They know the price of everything and the value of nothing.'

'Oh, do they?' he asked softly. 'Well, I know your price, sweetheart; I have yet to decide whether I'm buying.'

Pushing himself to his feet, he towered above her, six feet of lean male. Her face mirrored her perplexity. She didn't quite know what he meant by that last statement but she didn't think he made empty threats.

'We'll start at the National Gallery,' he suggested, clearly thinking he was on a wild-goose chase. 'I'll enjoy a day of culture accompanied by a beautiful woman. What you'll get out of it I can't think.'

It was on the tip of her tongue to say 'sore feet' but she didn't think it would help to antagonise him further. Some small part of him wanted to believe her despite his hard-bitten exterior. She also knew he despised the inclination to trust her. She had never wanted to prove her integrity so deeply and she wordlessly complied with his wishes, preceding him out of the room.

Knowing that if Derek had said he was going away for the weekend he would not be touring his usual haunts, Lauren saw the day's activity as futile. She expected her brother to return after the weekend without a suspicion of what was facing him. She told Ryan this as they were walking along the Embankment near the Thames.

'So it's all a coincidence?' He slanted a mocking glance at her, aware of her shivering under the influence of the cold easterly wind.

'Yes.' Her confidence in her brother was impressive and, seeing it was pointless to argue, he summoned the car.

'Where to next?' He was relentless. Purpose emanated from him. 'Want to go home?'

Lauren blinked. 'Home?'

'Your flat, remember? Getting used to Mayfair? You acclimatise quickly.'

Lauren regarded him with dislike. 'If you remember——' she was frosty '—you declared my home out of bounds.'

'Only if you were on your own. I guarantee you'll be safe with me.' The look she gave him made Ryan Daniels smile. 'What danger do you sense in me, Lauren?'

The question was soft and yet it struck like a barb. Lauren met Ryan Daniels's eyes squarely, and wished she hadn't. She was used to masculine innuendo but there was something in his gaze that had a dangerous appeal.

'I suppose going back might be a little unnerving.' Ryan found her easy to comfort. He lifted a hand to stroke over her hair, finding the wealth of mahogany silk a seductive enticement.

'I'll be all right.' Lauren tried to block out the memory but lurking shadows remained. She became conscious of his fingers moving to caress her ear and the spell was

broken. 'Do you mind keeping your hands to yourself?'
Green eyes were alive with protest.

Ryan's mouth compressed mockingly and he put his
hands behind his back.

The journey to the flat was an uncomfortable one. At
least it was for Lauren. The enforced intimacy of the
confined space made her suddenly aware that she had
placed herself in the hands of a stranger. A stranger who
was potently masculine and used to being in control.
Ryan Daniels had joined her in the back seat, leaving
the driving to Mitch Harrison, and appeared perfectly
relaxed. Confident and assured, he had none of her
doubts about the future; he was full of purpose and
intent on stamping out any threat to the Daniels empire.
She wished she possessed a fraction of his sureness. All
she had to cling on to was her own pride and her ab-
solute belief in her brother's honesty.

Catford looked rather shabby after the environs of
Mayfair, and she was surprised Ryan Daniels had deigned
to accompany her. He was probably expecting to find
Derek hiding under the bed. She led the way to the first-
floor flat, noting the empty, stained milk bottles left by
one of the other residents and the litter of leaflets and
throw-away papers that no one had claimed just inside
the door. She usually cleared those away herself; no one
had bothered that morning. Lauren was discomfited by
the critical feelings she had developed towards her home,
and wished Ryan Daniels had stayed in the car with the
driver.

As soon as she reached the landing just below her
apartment a cold feeling prickled down her spine. Ryan
pushed past her, clearing the remaining three stairs and
fingered the splintered wood around the lock.

'Go back to the car,' he ordered.

'No!' she refused, receiving an impatient look as she took the initiative and pushed past him. A sob broke from her lips. The flat had been their haven. When their parents had died leaving Derek, at nineteen, the head of the family, he had given up his university degree to provide Lauren with a home when she had told him how uncomfortable she felt with the people who had fostered her.

Swallowing hard, she took in the devastation. The apartment was in chaos—years of precious endeavour maliciously destroyed and broken.

'I'm sorry.' Ryan's voice came quietly from behind her.

'Well, you should be!' Lauren stamped her foot, tears trickling from her eyes. 'If you'd let people know you'd retrieved those documents...or whatever they were, none of this would have happened.'

'No,' he agreed, reaching out to brush her damp cheek, his jaw tightening as she slapped his hand away. 'You would have been implicated in theft and the villains would have gone to ground.'

'So you've caught them, have you?' She was scathing, her eyes hot with temper.

'I'm working on it.'

She dismissed his remark as masculine bravado, too appalled by the destruction confronting her. She swallowed a sob, sitting down on the edge of a chair. Covering her face with her hands, she tried to grasp the enormity of it all. Where would it end? First the espionage, then Derek's disappearance, her car and now her home.

'Was there anything irreplaceable?' he asked.

He sounded like an insurance man! Lauren's hands fell from her face, her fury reaching unknown heights.

'Yes. Security. My home—peace of mind—everything that makes this place somewhere I can shut out the world!' She threw the words like stones. 'I don't suppose you can imagine that, can you? You probably change residences on a weekly basis, any problems solved by signing a cheque. Well, you can't pay for any of this. It will never be the same!'

Ryan Daniels pushed his hands into his pockets, watching her as if she were a strange new species. Glancing around the room, he thought he could restore it to its former state for a little under ten thousand. Most of the stuff was chain-store.

'What the hell——?' A cushion hit him a glancing blow followed by an alarm clock which, fortunately for him, he ducked.

'Get out of here!' She advanced with a broken chair-leg.

'Put that down!' he commanded impatiently. 'I realise you're upset but——'

'You don't realise,' she yelled at him. 'You live in a different world. You, Ryan Daniels, have no idea!'

His hand came up with lightning speed and caught the piece of wood she was wielding more as a statement than with any attempt to harm.

She let go, her shoulders slumping, her whole demeanour one of defeat. The dark uncertainties of the past arose before her like a dark wave and she put her hands up to shield her face defensively.

Ryan Daniels responded instinctively, curling his hand around the back of her neck and bringing her into the shelter of his embrace. He felt as if he were comforting the burglar, because her particular rope had broken. Her scent drifted to his nostrils and Ryan bent his head, feeling the cool silk of her hair brush his cheek.

'The door will be fixed in a few hours. I'll get a security system in place by tomorrow. They won't come back. What they want isn't here—they know that now.'

'They want me,' she whispered into his chest. 'They think I know where the papers are.'

'Don't worry; they won't openly challenge me. Besides, you're going to be hard to find.' Ryan's hand was warm against her nape. 'Do what I tell you and you'll be perfectly safe.'

His self-confidence was like a fire on a cold night, drawing Lauren with all the frailty of insecurity towards him to bask in the reflected warmth.

'I don't know anything about this.' She raised her head to beseech him, 'I wish you'd believe me.'

Ryan's eyes narrowed on hers, his blue eyes with that knife of silver cutting into her. 'I do believe you. I believe you can conjure up a summer haze over a swaying field of wheat. Beautiful women have the power of illusion and you're more beautiful than most.'

She pulled away, the moment of warmth lost, glaring resentfully at him.

Mitch Harrison was summoned and told to stay until the repairs had been done. Ryan then urged her out of the flat, down to the street entrance below. Lauren allowed him to lead her away from her home with the feeling nothing would ever be the same again.

He watched her as she gave a long backward glance, giving her a moment as he opened the passenger door.

'Time to move on,' he spoke quietly, but with a significance that didn't escape his companion.

With a haughty tilt of her head, she moved past him and allowed herself to be seated in the car. Ryan let his breath whistle through his teeth. Lauren Walsh, he decided, was a bundle of trouble. Surprisingly, however, the thought didn't deter him. Something had gone drastically wrong with his life if a beautiful thief could make him break every rule in the book to help her. She was an ungrateful wretch too; she almost made him feel guilty.

'How do you feel about a Caribbean cruise?' he asked in a throw-away tone.

Lauren gazed at him speechlessly. 'Is that your idea of a joke? How could I possibly leave London?'

'How can you possibly stay?' Ryan murmured, putting the conversation on ice as he manoeuvred the limousine back into the traffic.

Lauren felt caught on the horns of a dilemma. Ryan Daniels was entirely serious about the Caribbean cruise. Apparently, his family spent several weeks a year on their yacht, *Halcyon*, and they were to depart just as soon as his mother Lady Daniels and her daughter Penelope returned from a shopping spree in Paris.

Lauren had refused point-blank to entertain the idea of the cruise, but the alternative, being left alone in London, hadn't much to recommend it either. She comforted herself that Derek would return come Monday morning and the nightmare would end.

Sir Charles Daniels viewed Lauren's addition to the household as a romantic whim of his son's, and in the role of Ryan's newly acquired girlfriend she had less explaining to do than might be imagined. Ryan had explained about the burglary and her fear of returning to the flat, and Sir Charles had accepted this version of the truth, appearing pleased with his son's supposed chivalry.

When Ryan excused them both from that evening's dinner, the older man regarded them benignly, alerting Lauren to the fact that something else was going on that she didn't know about. Wealthy, well bred families could be expected to show a little cynicism when the son and

heir brought home a damsel in distress, but instead she
sensed hopeful approval.

'That went all right, I think,' Ryan remarked as he
held the car door open for her. 'Now dinner. Where
would you like to go?'

She shifted across the seat, trying to escape any contact
with his body. 'I haven't much of an appetite,' she said.

'Maybe not. But we need to talk. If Derek doesn't
return as you predict, we'll need to know something
about each other. My father might accept your sudden
appearance in my life; my mother is a little more astute
in personal matters.'

Lauren felt that the less she knew about Ryan Daniels
the better it would suit her. Her features were quite revealing on this point. A muscle clenched in Ryan's jaw
and Lauren guessed she wouldn't have to do much to
qualify as the most irritating female of his acquaintance.

'I can jot down a life history if you like. It won't take
long. I'm twenty-three. So far it's been school, college,
fashion design and modelling. There you are—you're up
to date.'

'Mario's,' he instructed the driver. Ryan Daniels took
little notice of Lauren's exasperated sigh and relaxed
against the upholstery, negligently observing the area they
were passing through.

'I don't like it when you make people think we're involved.' Lauren frigidly brought up the familiarity he
had adopted towards her, realising she wasn't going to
be allowed to get out of dinner.

Ryan Daniels turned his head to regard her lazily.
'Why?'

'Well, we're not!' Her tone wondered at his ob-
tuseness in face of the obvious.

'No,' he agreed patiently as if talking to a simpleton.
'But it would seem the least complicated way of ex-

plaining your presence in my family home. Explaining to my parents that I'm offering you protection from a gang of thieves who presume you're in possession of industrial secrets belonging to Daniels and Blackthorn might make the atmosphere a little strained.'

'Even worse if you suggested I was under some form of house arrest.'

Ryan considered this. 'You came to me. I let you go, if you remember.'

She conceded this grudgingly. Ryan had a way of taking what she considered quite justified protests and making them sound churlish and ungrateful. If Derek had somehow become entangled in the affair, then they would both owe Ryan Daniels a debt of gratitude for his patience. She realised he could quite easily wash his hands of the whole business and hand over what he had already got to the police.

It was a considerably chastened Lauren who sat across the table from Ryan Daniels in a small but exclusive Italian restaurant.

'Tell me about the fashion world. How did you get into modelling? You say you trained in design?' he asked.

'Yes.' Lauren picked up her glass of Frascati and sipped it appreciatively. 'It's a capricious way to make a living. I had a friend whose financial backing was sounder than mine. I modelled her clothes and it started from there.'

'Anyone I know? The friend,' he specified, and she blinked, suspicious of his interest.

'Marisa Lasalle. Her father is Paul Lasalle, he——'

'I know him. Good, we're making progress.' The waiter arrived and he ordered for both of them, merely pausing to make sure she had no violent objection to his choice. It appeared they were to have the house speciality, which was a seafood pasta concocted by the great Mario himself.

When the waiter had gone, those light, analytical eyes turned on her again. Lauren received the impression he found her puzzling.

'Your apartment. It meant a lot to you, didn't it? You're only young, not long out of college. Homes usually take on sanctuary status when life has been hard. Has life been hard for you, Lauren?'

Startled, her emerald eyes were unknowingly revealing. 'Not so hard I would take to crime, Mr Daniels.'

'That wasn't what I meant—no matter, I can see it's a sensitive area; we'll leave that for now. Tell me about college; did you go out of London or stay at home?'

She had attended a London college, although good courses had been available elsewhere. For most young people further education was more than a diploma or degree—it involved going to a strange town or city and starting again from scratch. For the first time she wondered if she had been a burden to her brother. He had never complained but then Derek wouldn't; he took his responsibilities very seriously. At eighteen, she hadn't been ready to start again. It had only been three years since her parents' death and the unfortunate placing with a foster family.

'I like London. Do you find that significant?' Her beautiful face was alight with challenge.

'No.' He regarded her through narrowed eyes, a slight frown drawing his brows together. 'A home-bird and yet anything but a plain little sparrow in front of the camera. What do you think of to get such power in those shots? It certainly wasn't tractors.' He allowed himself a small grin, watching her indignation grow.

'I think about what the photographer tells me to think about. What has that got to do with convincing your mother that we're seeing each other?' she asked.

'Nothing. I was merely curious.' He was laughing at her again and she almost threw her wine at him. 'What a bundle of contradictions you are. You'd fight me to the death to protect your brother, but you wouldn't leave home to go to college.'

Lauren glared at him through a film of tears. She didn't want to cry in front of him again. Observing her silently for a few moments, Ryan Daniels relented. He took over the onus of self-revelation.

'I'm thirty-five.' He copied her style of documenting her life but his eyes were teasing rather than unkind. He continued with a predictable list of public schools through to graduating from Oxford. He had worked for various companies before stepping into a managerial post in the Daniels Corporation. His achievements were impressive both academically and in the business world but it told her nothing more of him than a typed c.v. Lauren guessed his personal life was as blank as her own—not because as in her case he had never indulged in any depth of intimacy, but because for Ryan Daniels nobody had counted for much.

Expanding on this intuition, she showed an interest in him for the first time. 'Wouldn't I get in your way on the cruise? Having a girlfriend can be a bit of a disadvantage, especially in our circumstances. I'd cramp your style.'

'Not really.' his eyes lingered on the generous curves of her mouth, moving on to appreciate the dark, luxuriant texture of her hair, the tongues of candle-light highlighting the auburn tints. He thought her exquisite and didn't attempt to hide his admiration. 'My father has been making some heavy-handed hints, suggesting it's time I settled down. I have so far struck every prospective candidate off the list, so——' he made a speaking gesture with his hands '—I'd like to spend a few weeks in the sun without the odious task of pretending to court some young, frivolous rich thing who fancies herself in love with the Daniels empire.'

Lauren felt a degree of enlightenment. Sir Charles, she suspected, had given up hope of seeing his son smitten by anyone of his own social standing and was widening his horizons.

'You don't seem the type to have your future dictated; I would guess money and power are involved somewhere along the line,' she said.

Ryan Daniels lifted his glass to her in acknowledgement of the accuracy of her comment but expanded no further.

The meal wasn't exactly a great success. Lauren's appetite failed to return and her companion didn't eat much either. She didn't like to dwell on the reason for that but the sensual appreciation that absorbed her every expression and gesture made her feel as if she was being contemplated for dessert!

She sat beside him in the expensive limousine as they headed back towards the Mayfair residence, her face turned pointedly towards the window.

'Why do you find male appreciation so threatening, Lauren?' His voice made her jump and she glanced towards the driver, realising he couldn't hear through the glass that separated them.

'Appreciation?' She flashed a fighting glance at him. 'You've made me feel as if I were included on the menu.'

A slight smile touched his mouth. 'I would have booked every table if you were.'

'Let's not get this charade out of context, Mr Daniels. I am not and do not intend to be your girlfriend——'

'Lover is the word you're looking for,' he supplied calmly, watching the heat run into her cheeks. 'And don't be so sure. If you come out in a rash when I look at you, touching should be quite something.'

'You live in a fantasy world,' she flung at him, turning her shoulder on him and staring out into the dark night. Her heart was pounding against her ribs and she had to fight to even out her breathing. If she ever let this infuriating man touch her, she would despise herself until the end of time.

Lauren was relieved when they cruised through the gates of the Daniels mansion and she allowed Ryan to escort her into the house without speaking a word.

Sir Charles invited them into the study, the tradition of brandy and cigars for the men being relaxed in a gentlemanly effort to include Lauren. She equally politely allowed them their retreat, meaning to go straight to bed. The day, she felt, had been quite long enough. Bannister, the butler, waylaid her.

'There's a call for you, Miss Walsh,' he informed her, looking down his long nose. He showed her the way to a small living-room that she was informed was used by Lady Daniels. The room was warm and although elegant was cosy as well. The walls were pale yellow, with well preserved white cornices that bespoke Victorian origins. A waterfall of curtain material, gold-fringed, elaborately swagged and tailed, framed a wide bay window. A carved wooden surround to the fire with inlaid tiles continued the Victorian influence but the convincing flames in the hearth were actually supplied by gas, saving the beautiful décor of the room from the ravages of smoke. Comfortable two-seater couches offered ample seating space in pale grey and green, and Lauren sank down into one, trying to disguise her eagerness from the manservant who was lingering by the door.

'Thank you,' she dismissed him, and watched him go with a feeling of relief.

Her hopes were met, the sound of her brother's voice making her splutter into speech.

'Derek! Where are you? Are you all right?'

'Yes. Look, I'm sorry you've got mixed up in all this. Stay where you are. I'm going to prove to Daniels that I'm not guilty——'

'Derek! I can't stay here. Ryan Daniels wants me to join his family on a cruise. They're going to the Caribbean and—— Derek? Derek, are you there?'

There was a moment's silence when she thought they had been cut off. 'Good. That's a good idea.' Derek sounded as if he was thinking quickly. 'You'll be safe with him——'

'Don't you dare hang up——' Lauren groaned deep in her throat, pushing her dark hair back from her forehead and pausing mid-action when she saw Ryan Daniels leaning back against the door.

'What did he say?' he queried in an ominously quiet tone.

'He said he was going to prove his innocence.' She returned his gaze, pure frustration making her immune to the commanding quality therein. 'He—he also seems to think I should stay with you.'

Ryan Daniels could see that suggestion hadn't pleased her. 'Why doesn't he come to see me if he's innocent?' He expelled his breath impatiently. 'He's got the nerve to expect me to protect you after he's put you at jeopardy——'

'He hasn't! It's all some dreadful misunderstanding!'

'Your brother understands enough to keep out of my way. But then——' his gaze became assessing '—I have only your word for what he said to you.'

Lauren's green eyes widened at the accusation. 'If I were the criminal mastermind you think, I'd hardly come to you for help, would I?'

'Wouldn't you?' He approached her and Lauren gained her feet in one lithe movement, aware of the menace in him. Her fingers splayed against his shoulders to keep him at a distance, her eyes viridian as they challenged the storm in his gaze.

'The company grapevine must be in its death throes if speculation wasn't high about my interest in you. I spent enough time watching you work to keep them busy for weeks. I find it hard to believe you're the only one who didn't know I wanted you.'

Lauren swallowed drily, feeling unaccountable breathless. 'No, I didn't know,' she spoke huskily, 'but I do now. This isn't going to work, is it? I'd better go.'

'Where?' He raised an eyebrow mockingly. 'Nothing's changed. As long as you play by my rules, you'll have a choice in whatever you do.'

'Why doesn't that sound reassuring?' Locked in his gaze, she felt as if he read every thought in her head. But that was impossible; if he had that power he would know she was innocent. 'What does playing by your rules mean?' She tossed her head back, trying to break the spell he had over her.

'It means don't tempt me by putting yourself at my mercy.' Long fingers caressed her throat before she flinched away from him. 'I don't think I have to explain that to you, do I?'

'I thought you liked your women willing,' she reminded him of his own words and felt a frisson of excitement dance through her veins at the knowledge in his eyes.

'There's a fine distinction,' he told her, his voice ensnaring her. 'There's willing because you want something and there's willing when you just can't help yourself.'

Lauren didn't ask him to explain that; it was there in the sureness of his smile, in the warm heat of his gaze. Despite her protests, a spark of attraction drew life inside her.

'You can count on my co-operation.' Bravado kept her from running from the room. She turned on her heel, her back straight and proud, denying the threat he embodied. If only she could cool her blood so easily. Dimly, Lauren was beginning to understand the mysteries of sexual attraction; it was without rhyme or reason, the primal urges of life had a logic all of their own, and it was her misfortune that she should become vulnerable to such mysteries when all else in her life was in chaos.

CHAPTER THREE

MONDAY morning came and went, Lauren's hopes of her brother's speedy return fading as the week progressed. Lady Daniels and her daughter returned to London and Lauren found herself reluctantly involved in plans for the forthcoming cruise.

When Ryan Daniels took out his cheque-book to provide her with expenses, she took great pleasure in shredding the cheque.

'It's a bit late for the high moral scene, isn't it?' His voice sliced into her. 'Since you're my partner, I'd rather you didn't look cheap.'

'I design my own clothes, Mr Daniels.' Her chin lifted proudly. 'Every item will be original. I don't imagine I'll find it difficult to live up to your standards.' Her scorn was equal to his attempt to ridicule her and a smile curled his mouth, but it didn't look friendly.

'I suppose the cruise will provide you with the perfect shop window. Some of the female guests are extremely influential.'

'It would really upset you if I proved to be innocent, wouldn't it?' Lauren was incensed that he should misread her every motive.

'Not at all. It would restore my faith in human nature.' His tone left her in no doubt that he considered the likelihood extremely remote.

Giving up on the argument, Lauren returned with him to her flat to retrieve the necessary items. The apartment had been tidied and the door repaired. A complex alarm system had been installed and she watched Ryan programme it with an expertise that drew her reluctant admiration.

Leaving him to it, she went to her room to pack up the summer collection she had designed. Most of the dresses had been ordered by clients and she would have to work hard to replace them when she returned. She had no intention of letting Ryan buy her clothes. When the reckoning came, she wanted nothing to complicate the picture. Lauren wanted justice, and involved in that was this man's abject apology.

He entered the room, ignoring her outraged glare, his eyes sweeping over the feminine décor. She doggedly returned to her task, her movements suddenly agitated, her shoulders tense and her skin heating to such a degree that she felt stifled.

'You'd feel better if we made love.' His voice sounded matter-of-fact, and Lauren wasn't sure whether she'd heard right. When she turned to take in his hateful presence, he held up a bedraggled furry toy. 'This must have sentimental value; you wouldn't keep it for its good looks.' Passing it to her, he viewed her confusion with amusement. 'Any time you feel like graduating——'

'Will you please leave my bedroom?' Her green eyes sparked with repressed fury. 'And for your information I'd rather die than swap Peggit for you.'

Peggit, like many of her most treasured possessions, was something salvaged from her childhood. The small, one-eared bear was almost shiny with the occasional tuft of fluff.

'You know how to kill a man's ego.' He moved to the door but his eyes goaded her. 'But for your ongoing education good sex is much more interesting than novels, cocoa or a bald little bear.' Winking at her, he murmured, 'Hurry up,' and left her speechless.

It was with a monumental effort that Lauren calmed herself to meet the combined interest of the Daniels family at dinner that evening.

Elizabeth, Lady Daniels was a beautiful woman. She had exquisite bone-structure and bore her years easily. Her hair was silver-blonde, worn in a pleat, and her eyes were blue with a definite twinkle in their depths. Penelope, unlike Ryan, did not resemble her mother. She had dark hair, almost black eyes and appeared to embrace Lauren's inclusion on the Caribbean cruise with a rather surprising enthusiasm.

Ryan Daniels watched his family's reception of the orphan in their midst with barely concealed curiosity. Whereas his usual well bred, wealthy girlfriends set the fur flying, Lauren appeared to fit in rather harmoniously. The feeling that she was just what he was looking for was only marred by the business with her brother. If it weren't for that, he would have a mutually beneficient contract drawn up whereby he would fund her fashion ambitions and she would fulfil the requirements of a wife. Lauren's occasional burst of temper he allowed as a minus but, considering her personal attributes, he thought he might enjoy the occasional spat.

Aware of being watched, Lauren flicked him a glance across the dinner table. Resentment glittered in her eyes. She was ill suited to captivity however glamorous the cage.

Delicately slicing the delicious sole in hollandaise sauce she had chosen, Lady Daniels sympathised over the damage to Lauren's car and the subsequent robbery.

'You must be looking forward to getting away, my dear. What bad luck.'

'I think it's awful!' Penelope Daniels's eyes burned into Lauren's. 'I'd be a nervous wreck if it happened to me.'

'It has been a strain.' Lauren looked to Ryan for guidance. She realised she should be saying something about his being wonderfully supportive but the words stuck in her throat.

'Fortunately, Lauren had the good sense to come here. It would have been rather traumatic if she'd had to remain in the apartment.'

'You've been very kind.' Lauren's eyes skidded to Sir Charles, whose help she found easier to appreciate.

'Not at all,' he retorted with bluff charm. 'You're a delight on the eye, my dear. Ryan and I have enjoyed your company.'

Smiling her thanks, Lauren was conscious that she was the subject of approving interest from the Daniels family but not, she intuitively felt, for the same reasons. Penelope Daniels appeared keen to have her as a friend. Lady Daniels was as gracious a hostess as her husband was host, showing not the slightest suspicion that she was a gold-digger after her son's money.

Embarking on the first leg of their journey to the Caribbean was, in the circumstances, less of an ordeal than Lauren had anticipated. The company jet flew the Daniels contingent into Antigua. It was a long journey, but the jet was eminently luxurious. Lauren found she slept for most of the flight, only wakening when Ryan shook her gently and told her to fasten her seatbelt.

Antigua had a familiar international flavour, with its airport, shopping mall, boutiques and harbour for the major cruise lines. Sunshine washed everything in brilliance, the sky cobalt-blue with small cotton-wool clouds, the sea a blend of turquoise and aquamarine.

'I hope you've brought a bikini.' Ryan's hand slid to rest above her hip, his fingers warm through the thin cotton top she wore.

'Why?' she queried in an undertone, troubled by the intimacy he affected in public.

'My imagination is restricted to your more revealing publicity shots.'

'You are a reptile,' she murmured under her breath.

'No, I'm a man. You appear to be unfamiliar with the species.'

'I hope my luck holds.' She smiled sweetly.

'I wouldn't count on it.' He smiled blandly into the vexed emerald of her gaze.

'Ryan,' his mother called him, indulgence in her tone. '*Halcyon*'s moored over there, can you see?'

He viewed Lauren's astonishment as she took in the size of the cruiser. 'What did you expect, a rowing boat?' he asked.

The *Halcyon* was a sizeable cruiser rather than the luxury yacht Lauren had expected. There were to be forty guests with about fifteen crew members. Antigua was the initial and final stage of the cruise. They were to head west to Virgin Gorda, and spend a week island-hopping around the Virgin Islands, including St John's, St Thomas and St Croix, before returning once more via St Kitts to Antigua.

Ryan showed her to her cabin. It was a mixture of luxury and convenience and reflected the expectation of sun-bleaching heat. Light colours and a large, slowly revolving fan bespoke a vessel used to sun-spangled seas, not the bleak wind-chill of the Atlantic.

'I'll leave you to bemoan your fate,' Ryan mocked her. 'If it weren't for me you could be huddled in front of the fire, listening to the rain.'

'If it weren't for you, I'd appreciate the change of scenery,' she returned flippantly.

His silver-blue eyes showed something fleetingly like admiration. It made her wonder at the sort of women he usually partnered—but she supposed he was a big enough prize to warrant undiluted simpering from any aspiring deb who set her cap at him.

Unpacking, she hung up her latest creations, the light, filmy designs that had seemed ludicrously insubstantial in London, totally right for the heat of the Lesser Antilles.

It was a pleasant room . . . cabin, she corrected herself, looking around. She had expected a bunk-bed and cramped quarters. Instead, she had a sizeable divan with a froth of snowy white pillows and a cover that mixed cotton and lace in a cool, decorative effect. The carpet was a hard-wearing weave, the colour of bamboo. Teak doors concealed adequate shelving as well as somewhere to hang her more perishable clothes.

Locking the door, Lauren threw off her clothes and made for the small shower compartment. Turquoise tiles and a frosted glass door enhanced the seafaring atmosphere, as did the gentle movement of the ship as it moved out of harbour. It had been a long journey and she was glad to let the cool spray freshen her skin.

Drenching her hair, Lauren found her mind straying to the tall, authoritative figure of Ryan Daniels. She was torn between emotions of resentment and gratitude. He had provided a safe haven when her world had been threatened and yet his hunt for her brother made him her protector and persecutor at the same time. Then there was the role of his fictitious girlfriend that she had to adopt, which was designed to fool his family and various predatory females who were after his money. On top of which she reluctantly felt physically aware of the man, increasingly so as their subterfuge demanded they feign a level of romantic attachment. So far she had channelled her distress over the espionage business into a prickly, abrasive attitude that kept him at bay. If he sensed weakness . . . Lauren pushed her hair back from her face. Her mind shied away from predicting the result.

She pondered over her dress for the evening. By now the female contingent on the *Halcyon* would gather that Ryan had been pirated by some aspiring model and, deciding to dress the part, she picked a dress that was utterly female, slinky and body-hugging in emerald water silk. She would never have designed it with herself in mind. It tempted and challenged at the same time and clashed dramatically with the cool reserve she normally aspired to. The cunning design showed a modest degree of cleavage, left her shoulders bare but had a halter-neck and bands of material across her arms as a pretence of respectability. Barbaric gold earrings completed the ensemble. She felt like going barefoot but found a suitable pair of stilettos that would probably sink the ship.

She fitted in rather well, she reflected, having endured Ryan's gaze in a slow drag over her body. More money than dress sense abounded, so too an exotic display of jewels.

That evening, she sampled Caribbean cuisine and surveyed her fellow guests. The food was West Indian with influences from a mixture of cultures that had held sway over the islands. Lobsters, red snapper, kingfish, conch strips sautéed in herbs and garlic, chicken deep-fried with a selection of vegetables; sweet potato, bread fruit, okra and the ubiquitous avocado dip.

The guests were a cosmopolitan blend of European nations, with the exception of the Van Dykes, an American family, the head of whom, John Van Dyke, ran the American subsidiary of Daniels and Blackthorn, responsible only to Ryan Daniels who was at present managing director.

The Rabanne family provided a sizeable contingent. Jean-Paul and Marie-Louise Rabanne were the epitome of elegant snobbery and their offspring Chantal and Chloe appeared willing to carry on the family tradition. Luc Rabanne, the son and heir, was a little more human. He was clearly a charmer and the warm glances his Gallic eyes sent in Lauren's direction suggested he was willing to excuse her lack of pedigree.

Richard Harrington was seated beside Penelope Daniels, his clean-cut good looks a little too perfect, his manners impeccable to the point of parody. She sensed she was being watched and found that Ryan had been taking an interest in her reactions.

'I'll guide you through the menu if you like,' he responded to her questioning glance.

'I am familiar with some of the dishes,' she said, asserting her independence. 'If you could just point out anything that might be dangerous.' She kept up the pretence they were talking about the food.

'"One man's meat . . ."' he quoted softly. 'Don't women enjoy a little danger?' His eyes held hers for a moment in intimate communication.

'Not me,' she denied, suddenly uncomfortable with his playful mood, and dragged her gaze away from his, unaware of the softening of her mouth and the dilation of her pupils. She created a magnetism she was barely aware of, attracting secretive, speculative glances from many of the males around the dining table, as they instinctively sensed the sensual awakening taking place in the woman.

They were dancing, with the soft breeze wafting in from the sea, and Lauren's eyes flickered over Ryan as he drew her to him when the music slowed down to a lazy, sensual rhythm. His white dinner-jacket moulded his wide shoulders, his linen and ribbon tie perfect. She wondered if he ever had to hunt through his wardrobe for something to wear or if some unseen hand put together complementary outfits, immaculate in every detail.

'I don't quite understand the dress.' His voice against her ear surprised her. 'Is it one of your collection?'

'Don't you like it?' She lifted eyes that didn't give a damn to his face.

'Yes.' His slight smile was derisive. 'It was designed with a man in mind, wasn't it? It's not you . . . or at least not the Lauren Walsh I know.'

'But then you don't know me very well,' she pointed out coolly. 'What did you expect me to wear?'

'A hair shirt,' he muttered, looking past her to survey the other guests and then smiled down into her eyes as she tried valiantly not to respond to his humour. 'It's an improvement.'

Undoubtedly everyone aboard considered her Ryan Daniels's latest toy. She cast him a resentful look from between dark silken lashes as he lay beside her, his skin golden, his hair sleek and gilded by the brilliance of the sun. She had speculated that in the scant attire of a Caribbean cruise he would turn out to be pale and shapeless. But she had the living denial inches from her, his body every bit as classically fashioned as his well bred business self.

She tried to picture him totally abandoned in a woman's arms and then blinked quickly to destroy the image, for the woman was her, and Ryan—Ryan was devastating!

Lauren found this sudden rush of physical attraction had a power that shocked her. At the tender age of fifteen she had had to cope with her parents' death and being fostered with a family who were strangers to her. She had stayed with them six months, during which time she had been aware of a growing level of intimacy being directed at her by the head of the family, John Patten. She had made great efforts not to be alone in the house with him and had finally run away when he had 'accidentally' come into the bathroom while she was in the shower. The memory still scalded her with embarrassment.

Ever since the reality of having her privacy violated so young in life she had felt unmoved by the men who had been attracted to her. Their hot eyes and eager hands had repulsed her and she had presumed sexual excitement was something she was not going to experience. She had presumed wrong!

Her skin goose-bumped as Ryan sat up, the skin drawing tightly over his ribcage. He oiled his arms, the smell and slick surface it gave his skin drying up her mouth. She wondered what he'd think if he knew what images were rioting through her mind.

Turning her face away, she let the dazzle of the sun on the pool fill her gaze with blue and gold. Beautiful creatures swam and lay like sardines around the square of water, the occasional outsize or potato shape belonging very much to the business acquaintances and unlucky rich kid who had designer everything except the body and face to match. She supposed many of the glamorous young things were like herself—decorations for a rich man's table.

'Sometimes, Lauren,' Ryan's voice silked against her ear, 'I almost hear you thinking.'

The concept appalled her but she ignored him, even when he let a drip of oil drop on to her shoulder and began to rub it in with the tip of one indolent finger.

'Every man here envies me.' He spoke softly, a musical, sing-song note to his voice that mocked his words.

'You wouldn't find it very hard to find a rich man to indulge your ambitions. You have excellent collateral.'

'Ryan!' Her protest came as he used the oil to allow his finger to glide along her spine.

'"Ryan",' he mimicked. 'How could I possibly shock you in front of all these people?'

It wasn't so much what he did, it was Lauren's reaction to it. Recognising the possibility of physical attraction had opened a floodgate of sensations. It upset her greatly and she didn't know what to do about it except attack the source.

The days that followed offered a sky and seascape of blue, broken by the moods of the sea and path of the sun. Lauren felt as if her bones were melting in the sun, her whole body caught up in the swaying, lilting ways of the Caribbean.

Halcyon's silken trail into the harbour of Virgin Gorda was met with mixed response. John Van Dyke and Richard Harrington were to head a party to Gorda Peak.

The languid pool-dwellers had decided on Little Dix Bay. Lauren had heard Chloe Rabanne talking about the exclusive resort as the only thing worth visiting. She wondered why, when the islands offered so much that was interesting and beautiful, the supposed sophisticates of the party looked for the nearest expensive boutique and cocktail bar the like of which was duplicated throughout the world.

Ryan chose neither of the options available; indulging Lauren's wish to explore, he suggested the Baths, an unassuming title for what resembled a palace tossed together by careless giants. Under the shadow of the rocks it was possible to wade and swim through clear waters lit by shafts of sunlight. The surreal atmosphere allowed Lauren to forget for a time the troubles in her life and twist and turn into the lapping caress of the water, her hair fanning out behind her in a dark cloud. The tall, masculine figure she was becoming increasingly familiar with arrowed in the water not far from where she floated in an effortless manner, his golden hair darkened by the water. She watched through narrowed lashes as he sliced through a jag of sunlight and his body was cast in liquid gold, his ribs arced as his arm cut into the water, a modern-day Apollo forging into the darkness as he disappeared into shadow, a trail of white froth in his wake.

'Show-off,' she muttered, trying to deny the awareness of his male beauty, but the water suddenly felt dangerous and she swam towards a shelf of rock bathed in brilliant golden light.

The turmoil in the water alerted her and she found herself reaching the edge of the rock only to find Ryan a stroke ahead of her, hauling himself out, water streaming down his body, his shoulders and arms gilded as the muscles bunched and eased when he turned himself around to look down at her. He was all light to her darkness and she turned and swam back into the shadows only to feel the force of his dive and feel his body arch under hers.

Hands seized her waist and she was hoisted up into the air then fell back into the water with a splash that had little grace to recommend it.

'You—swine,' she exploded, finding her feet and trying to push her hair out of her eyes. His laughter incensed her and she grabbed blindly at his arms as he appeared to be about to launch her into the air again.

'Don't you want me to let go?' He held her against his body, his breath hot against the wetness of her throat.

She didn't! There was nothing she wanted more than to relax against his hard, masculine body and let the water lap against them as they entwined. But, 'I want you to leave me alone,' she panted, dimly making out his features, her fingernails digging into his shoulders.

'I'm only playing, Lauren.' His voice left her in no doubt that he found her reaction interesting. 'You get restless when we sunbathe; I thought watersports might appeal to you.'

'How do you expect me to relax when my brother is in danger?' She peeled his hands off her waist, able to see him clearly now her eyes had adjusted. He was watching her, knowing that she was denying the attraction between them and curious about her lack of ease with him.

Allowing her to move away, Ryan was almost convinced she was inexperienced with men and called himself a fool for his gullibility. No woman that desirable could get to twenty-three without intriguing the male sex. Watching her swim away, he let his body sink below the water, glad of the cold depths to ease the ache of desire she evoked.

They joined up with the others in Little Dix Bay towards early evening, sun-kissed and hair tangled by the sea. The Rabannes and Sir Charles and Lady Daniels were perfectly groomed in comparison. Lauren's all-in-one white catsuit laced up at the front and left a great deal of spine showing, made decent by the fall of her hair, which the sea had created erotic havoc with. She exuded unconscious sexuality that made the exquisite Rabannes look like cosseted blooms with the waxy beauty of cultured flowers.

Ryan, too, looked like a beachcomber, wearing knee-length denim shorts and a blue and green T-shirt, dark glasses shielding his eyes as Chloe and Chantal flirtatiously rebuked him for daring to get sand between his toes.

Sipping a peach daiquiri, Lauren watched the sun gild the skies with a brilliant display of orange, pink and gold. There were definitely serpents in paradise—she heard their subtle hissing—but it was paradise! Catford in the rain seemed a poor comparison, but a pang of longing suddenly came over her for the safety of that old world that now seemed gone forever.

Ryan sat down beside her, stretching his long legs out and watching the surf crash on to the pretty little beach that provided an expensive backdrop for the rich who could afford it.

'Lauren, how could you expose your hair to the sea?' Chantal's voice purred over her, the woman coming to pose elegantly against the balcony rail. 'Your looks are your living, *n'est-ce pas?*'

Lauren fought hard not to laugh. Chantal certainly knew how to dish out an insult. She might not have said 'trollop' but it was in there somewhere.

'I do have other talents besides looking pretty.' Smiling in a relaxed fashion, she let her gaze drift over Chantal. 'I design clothes and jewellery. What do you do?'

Lauren thought she heard Ryan choke on his drink but, glancing sideways, she saw that his expression was blandly unforthcoming.

Sir Charles grinned. 'I think Lauren looks deliciously sun-kissed. Chantal works for several charities, don't you, dear?'

Chantal barely responded, her mouth decidedly sulky. It was left to Miles Van Dyke, the eldest of the Van Dyke offspring, to soothe her ruffled feathers. Barely out of college, he was young enough to show his adoration openly and Chantal allowed her wounded pride to find a haven.

'You're showing your claws, darling.' Ryan touched his glass to hers. 'A little of that goes a long way.'

'I didn't start it,' she muttered, her eyes flashing as they met his.

'She's French. I think something was lost in translation.'

'Thank goodness for that.' Lauren was unrepentant. 'If my fortune is my body, what does that make you?'

'A fortunate man?' he offered, smiling at her, glancing over at the rest of the party, who had drifted back into the interior of the bar as the breeze cooled. 'I think we should join them before that outfit becomes completely indecent.'

Lauren blushed to her hairline as he took off the dark shades and his eyes touched on the outline of her nipples against the thin material. Meeting the light quicksilver of his gaze, tension crackled through her as she realised he wasn't disapproving, his desire to have her less revealing being possessive in origin.

Later, when she got ready for dinner on the *Halcyon*, Lauren tried to analyse the increased sexual tension between Ryan and herself. He was the last person she wanted to feel this way about. She seemed to have no control over the riot of her emotions; even now, when she should be remonstrating with herself, Lauren felt a strange mixture of fear and elation. The unexpected stirrings of sexual desire made her restless, the burn in her body more than the captured heat of the sun.

Letting the towel that she had worn sarong fashion after her shower drop, she let the warm air drift over her skin as she chose a strapless dress in a native print that enhanced the coppery tan she had gained, her long, dark tresses loosely silking down her back. Wearing a musky perfume, she added golden bangles to her wrist and a pair of hooped earrings. Glancing in the mirror, she hardly recognised the creature confronting her.

The women she designed for were comfortable with their sexuality, some exploiting it. She caught the flavour of their desires when designing but had until then not appreciated the wish to flaunt her femininity in front of a male.

'Not me at all.' She tried to deny the fantasy character she had created.

Dredging up the image of her brother, she tried to keep in mind why she was on the cruise when Ryan turned to meet her resplendent in a white evening-jacket. His hair was brushed back in severe perfection, still slightly damp from the shower, and his white teeth tugged his lower lip in a considering manner as he surveyed her appearance with a warm glint in his eyes that clearly showed his approval.

'If you're trying to sell your designs it might be an idea not to alienate every female aboard.' Shaking his head slightly, he met her eyes for a moment with an intimate heat that made her knees quake.

Dinner was the usual exchange of the day's outings, including any gossip or snippets of news that had been picked up from the most recent newspapers that could be had. Lauren escaped as soon as she could, seeking the relative peace of the deck, gazing out at the spots of light on Virgin Gorda as the *Halcyon* moved out to sea.

It was hard to grasp the reality of what she had left behind. Here, with the menace of London hundreds of miles away, Lauren felt as if she'd escaped out of a nightmare. Derek was still in that nightmare, she reminded herself, shivering. The sun and pretty scenery didn't change that.

'Cold?' Ryan joined her, the smooth inner silk of his jacket sliding over her shoulders, encompassing her in his scent.

'A little. You don't have to join me; I'm just getting a breath of fresh air.'

He shrugged, following her gaze out to sea before returning to study her face, his eyes shadowed as he watched the breeze lift small tendrils of her hair in a capricious dance.

'What do you think of the Caribbean?'

'It's all very seductive.' She felt her spine stiffen, feeling as if she was keeping herself in check with every vestige of determination she possessed.

'It's supposed to be.' Leaning back against the rail, he watched the moon reflect in his champagne glass. 'Luxurious pampering for various business partners and customers.'

She tried to adopt his throw-away tone but found the relaxed lines of his body predatory, like a panther waiting for its prey to leave itself vulnerable.

'You'll pretend you've bought the moon next—or at least bribed it to shine so brightly,' she teased.

'I've hired a goddess,' he parried. 'Who needs the moon?'

Lauren met his eyes to discern his meaning. After Chantal's remarks she was sensitive about her position as his 'guest'.

'I haven't been hired,' she began hotly. 'No one pays for anything but my photographs, Mr Daniels.' She tried to move past him but slipped on a damp patch of the deck.

Ryan caught her and she fell against him, gathered into the warmth of his embrace. He had held her before when she was distressed over the robbery at her flat, but this was different. This time Lauren had nothing to distract her from the hard warmth of his body.

'If you can't take a compliment, I'm going to think you missed adolescence.' Ryan's voice had a thread of warm honey in the usual cultured tone, low and in-timate, and his breath feathered her temple.

'Let me go.' Lauren lowered her lashes, her heart raising its beat at their sudden proximity. She should be pushing him away, not letting her body curve into his. She tried desperately to remember that this man thought she was a thief, that he suspected her every motive, that he could quite easily ruin both herself and her brother.

'You don't sound as if you mean that.' His finger tilted up her chin, her lashes lifting to meet the undeniable affirmation of desire in his.

'The first time I saw you, you took my breath away. Do I have that effect on you, Lauren?'

'No,' she denied, trying to brave the seductive heat in his gaze.

'You panic when I get close.'

'I don't like you,' she returned, mesmerised by the firm lips hovering above hers.

'Liking isn't what I'm talking about. And you aren't moving.'

Before she could deny the implication of his words, his mouth captured hers in a firm, mind-blowing kiss. Lauren felt as if she was on a roller-coaster: her stomach flipped, her blood pounded through her veins, scorching beneath her skin, and her mouth developed a sensuality all of its own, sending pulses of excitement sizzling through her body.

His head lifted, his thumbs brushing her cheekbones, viewing the stunned, glazed emerald eyes with satis-faction, his fingers shaping her skull before his lips moved against the corner of her mouth, urging Lauren to let go of years of rigid control. Slavishly obeying, she let her mouth relax, feeling the warm, masculine lips shape themselves to hers and push them apart.

Her breath shuddered in her throat, her hands coming into contact with the warm heat of his skin through the thin cotton of his shirt. She could feel the hard rack of his ribs which she had watched oiled and baked gold in the sun, and of their own volition her hands slid over him, the lick of his tongue against hers making her jump with shock, but she was gathered closer, his jacket falling from her shoulders with a soft thud on to the deck. His hands gripped her hair, controlling her movements as his mouth marauded hers, not polite, not gentle but infinitely sexual, shredding her flimsy defences mercilessly.

'I've spent all day going crazy wanting to lick the salt off you.' His lips played with hers, before he exerted pressure on her hair and licked a trail of fire across her throat.

His words outraged and inflamed her in equal degrees. Lauren was shocked at the images he conjured up and she pushed at him as his teeth grazed her neck.

'Stop it! You have no right to——'

'What, kiss you?' Ryan controlled her struggles easily, watching her trying to disentangle herself with a lack of comprehension. He frowned, frustration evident in the hard glitter of his eyes. 'You wanted me to.'

'I—I—that's a lie.'

A slow smile curled his mouth at her apparent mortification. 'Just because we're cruising the Virgin Islands it doesn't mean you have to come out in sympathy. You may not believe in bed-hopping but I'm not falling for this act of Victorian purity——' His eyes swept over her. 'You just don't look the part.'

'I don't care what you believe,' she spat back at him, aware of the sound of people getting closer. 'As far as I'm concerned your judgement is way out.'

'Not in this.' His finger negligently traced her lower lip before she twisted her head away.

'Ryan?' Penelope Daniels called to him. 'John wants to know if you'll play poker.'

'Better than Trivial Pursuit.' Ryan let his gaze challenge Lauren, leaving her in no doubt that he had no time for women who teased and was unwilling to see her withdrawal in any other light.

Lauren let her breath out shakily. She'd had a narrow escape but the feeling of relief refused to come. Offering her heated skin to the sea breeze, she let her eyes close. If Ryan kept up the pressure, she was lost!

CHAPTER FOUR

LAUREN escaped to her cabin, feeling totally incapable of the social niceties expected when mingling with the Daniels's guests. How could Ryan desire her, suspecting she was a thief? Could a man want a woman physically and divorce the feeling from any vestige of liking or respect? Such questions spotlighted her own lingering fascination with the man. Was she beginning to care for him or was it merely lust?

'*Derek*!' She jumped as her brother emerged from the shadows of her cabin. 'What—what are you doing on board? If Ryan Daniels catches sight of you——'

'Shush!' Her brother halted the torrent of words. 'He won't have to see me if you broadcast it to the whole ship, will he?'

'You have a lot of explaining to do,' she maintained hardily. 'Do you know what's happened to the flat? I've been accused of industrial espionage! I'm scared to go home——'

'Shush,' Derek pleaded. 'I know it's been awful for you. I'm sorry. But it's been a shock for me as well.'

'A shock? How did those secrets get into your briefcase? Why did you ask me to pick it up?'

'My briefcase?' He looked as if something suddenly made sense. 'I wondered how Daniels was going to justify his accusation. I didn't know what was in there,' he explained hurriedly, coming into the light to see her confused gaze fixing on his hair.

His normally mousy-coloured hair was positively black and he appeared to be growing a moustache.

61

'What on earth are you playing at?' she exploded, feeling his seniority shrink and her own years multiply. 'Why didn't you wear a false nose and glasses...?'

'Don't laugh, Lauren. I don't want to be recognised until I can clear my name. You don't understand...' A soft knock at the door interrupted his explanation. 'I think it's Penny,' he informed her, shrinking back into the shadows.

'Penny?' Lauren frowned, viewing the door with suspicion.

'Penny Daniels,' he whispered.

'Penny Daniels,' she muttered, heading for the door. 'This had better be good.'

As promised, Penny Daniels stood there with the same hunted expression Derek wore. Together they told their story with supportive glances at each other, to Lauren's increasing sympathy.

Penny, it appeared, was trying to extricate herself from her engagement to Richard Harrington, whose practised charm had temporarily bemused her.

'He's just like Ryan,' Penny moaned. 'I couldn't marry a man like that, pursuing money and power with no feelings.'

Lauren felt for some reason she couldn't quite put her finger on that Penny was being a little unfair to her brother, but quickly dismissed the thought as she heard that Ryan was one of the possible suspects in the briefcase business.

'It had a present in it for Penny,' Derek revealed, looking adoringly at the girl. 'I wasn't particularly careful about hiding the combination number; it was taped inside my drawer. I never had anything valuable in it. I wanted the present for her birthday; that's why I asked you to pick it up.'

'So someone put the information in your briefcase. You said Ryan was a suspect. Why would he do that?' Lauren asked.

'To discredit me with Father,' Penny supplied. 'Richard is his rival for the presidency of Daniels and Blackthorn. If Ryan could tie me in with Derek and show that he was a thief, not only would the engagement to Richard be over but I would look gullible and cease to be a serious threat. Father wants grandchildren,' she revealed. 'Ruthlessness runs in the family. I don't know if Daddy would seriously use his influence to support his son-in-law in preference to Ryan, but my brother leaves nothing to chance. That's probably why Ryan has switched on the charm with you. If he appears to have a stable relationship, he's got the whole thing sown up.'

Lauren arched an eyebrow, remembering her skirmishes with Ryan. Charm, she thought, was the least of that man's persuasive talents.

'Ryan wants to talk to you,' Lauren quickly moved on. 'He's hushed up the espionage business. If he wanted to blacken your character, why would he do that? And then there's the damage to my car and the break-in at the flat.'

Derek and Penny didn't look convinced as they considered this.

'Our other suspect is Richard Harrington,' Penny informed her. 'He knows I want to break the engagement; he might be trying to get rid of Derek.'

It all sounded highly fanciful to Lauren's ears. She supposed years of being sensible must have had an erosive effect on her brother and he had deserted his usual sagacity in favour of some sub-standard mystery plot.

'Just suppose it was a genuine espionage attempt. You haven't helped by disappearing, Derek. I think you should see Ryan——'

'No!' They both looked horrified.

Frustrated, Lauren sat down on the bed. 'What are we going to do, then? I sympathise, but my position isn't exactly easy. Until we get this mess sorted out I can't go home and I'm under the dubious protection of someone you consider capable of framing an innocent man.'

They both looked rather crestfallen and Lauren tried to think of something they could do to improve the situation.

'Has either Ryan or Richard mentioned the incident to you, Penny?' she asked.

The other woman shook her head. 'I found out about the robbery from Father. He told me Ryan was trying to find one of his designers who'd gone missing. Derek had told me things had been tightened up of late because of security breaches, so we put two and two together. The design team's relatively small and none of the others had said they were going away.'

'I called Brian Taylor.' Derek named one of his colleagues. 'He said there was something going on, maybe another information leak, and Daniels wanted to see me.'

'Mummy found out through Bannister you were in the house and we guessed that Ryan was holding you until Derek returned,' Penny added.

'It wasn't quite like that,' Lauren demurred.

'When you said Ryan wanted you to come to the Caribbean, it seemed like a good idea to get you away from London. We didn't know whether Daniels had falsified those attempts at burglary to frighten you into staying under his protection or whether Harrington or whoever genuinely believed you to be in possession. Either way, you were better off on the *Halcyon* where I could be near you,' Derek finished his side of the story, his expression perplexed.

'So we're all here. What now?' Lauren queried. 'If Ryan's not to be trusted, what are we going to do?'

'Derek and I were going to search their rooms,' Penny said.

Lauren swallowed hard. She couldn't imagine what they expected to find; Ryan wasn't stupid and she didn't think Richard Harrington was either.

'Don't you think it's going to complicate things if Derek's found searching someone else's room?' she asked.

'We could do it,' Penny suggested.

'No!' Lauren put her foot down. 'If they're both innocent, we're no better than criminals searching through their things. I think we should face Ryan in front of Sir Charles and plead our case.'

Lauren had the distinct feeling her words were unwelcome and it wasn't hard to guess why. To be in the hands of some unknown, duplicitous force was unnerving. To have a bad plan of action was better than to have no plan at all other than throwing their fates into the hands of the master game-players. In face of determined opposition, Lauren suggested they all sleep on it before they did anything hasty.

She found the night's events left her restless and early the next morning she pulled on her swimming-costume and went for a swim in the pool. Pushing through the water, she felt the coolness stream past her ears, the sound of her breathing rhythmic and steady. Turning on to her back, she blinked the water from her eyes, staring up into the blue freshness of the morning sky, the space above giving her a sense of tranquillity denied through a long, sleepless night.

It was short-lived. She caught sight of Ryan sitting beside the pool, one of the waiters bringing a breakfast tray to his table.

'Can't sleep?' he enquired, as she hauled herself up on to the side, determined not to provide him with entertainment.

'Can't you?' she returned lightly, hoping for a quick escape. Picking up her towel, she was aware of his intrusive gaze, the water having moulded her costume to her body like a second skin.

Patting the chair beside him, Ryan commanded her to join him and, wrapping herself in a towelling robe, she complied reluctantly, tying her hair back in a ponytail.

'I only stay in bed if it's more interesting than getting up.' He watched the flicker of her lashes as she absorbed his meaning and refused to meet his eyes. 'I've been thinking about you all night. When you kiss, you don't set limits, then when it gets interesting you disappear behind all that puritanical indignation.' Looking thoughtful, he ticked off possibilities on his fingers. 'You haven't joined some holy order—the modelling cancels that out. You wouldn't be short of offers—that suggests a bad experience somewhere along the line. Did someone hurt you, Lauren? Is that why you scuttle for cover——?'

'When you try to use me for light relief?' she queried, her gaze suddenly accusing him. 'Why would I object to that, do you think?'

Ryan's eyes narrowed, a slight frown creasing his brow. 'You're hardly in a position to ask for commitment.'

She gave a breathless laugh. 'I'll ask for what I please and take no short measures. And for your information I'm not interested in a holiday romance while you play God with my future.'

'Last night it felt as if you could be persuaded.' His eyes were a mixture of cold Atlantic and warm Caribbean. 'Your body wants to play along; I suppose it's waiting for the cunning little mind to come up with an acceptable deal.'

'That sounds rather like a self-portrait, Ryan.' She stood up, her gaze flicking over him dismissively. 'If you'll excuse me, I need to shower.'

'Make sure it's cold.' Ryan's voice spoiled a magnificent retreat. 'You might last the day.'

She tried to pretend she didn't know what he was talking about but blushed all the same.

She was in the process of drying her hair when one of the stewards came into the room and then apologised upon seeing her. Lauren stilled as she watched him disappear from the room. Of course, the staff must have pass-keys! Derek could, at that very moment, be implicating himself further if he was found in either Ryan's or Richard Harrington's cabin.

Dressing hastily, she patrolled the ship looking for her brother. She couldn't see him anywhere and then she noticed the door of Ryan's cabin was slightly ajar. Ryan was still by the pool; she had caught sight of him on her search. Quietly, she opened the door and peeped inside. Derek was inside and she gasped at the sight of Ryan's possessions dumped on the floor from a series of drawers taken from their housing.

'Will you stop it?' she demanded, making her brother shoot to his feet. 'Get out of here now. If Ryan catches us, we have no chance of convincing him of our case. Are you crazy?'

'I have to do something, Lauren——'

'Not this. Go on, quickly—I'll sort this out.'

Derek looked dubious. 'What if he finds you? What then?'

'I doubt he'll prosecute,' she muttered, quickly inserting the drawer back on to its runners.

'Lauren——?'

'Just go!'

She heard his retreating footsteps as she continued with her task, neatly placing silk jockey shorts, socks and swimwear back into the drawers.

So intent was she on her rescue mission that she failed to hear the sound of another presence until the door closing made her jerk around.

Ryan quite deliberately locked the door and leant back against it, his eyes as sharp and cold as silver, the muscle in his jaw moving as he regarded her guilty expression.

'Lost something?' His voice cut into her like a whip.

Lauren glanced around the cabin searching for an escape route. There was none and the knowledge was reflected in her green eyes when they met the demand in his. The only explanation she could give was the truth, and she had no intention of revealing Derek's presence on the yacht.

'I hate to disappoint you but I don't hide my money under my mattress,' he said.

'I'm not a thief,' she maintained against all the evidence.

'So what are you doing here?' Ryan Daniels searched her beautifully tooled features as if he couldn't believe such an exquisite façade could disguise a consummate liar. 'I offered you expenses. Are you short of money?'

'No! I don't want your money, Ryan Daniels. I haven't taken anything. What are you going to accuse me of? Being caught in your cabin? Isn't that where people expect me to be?'

'You're not in court, Lauren.' His voice made her nerves jangle. 'You're with me.'

Apprehensive green eyes lifted to his. She remembered all too well his previous threats. He had warned her not to put herself in his power and here she was, helplessly caught.

Lauren swallowed drily, feeling suddenly hot. She stayed motionless while he approached with sheer effort of will.

'If it isn't money, what else did you expect to find? You can't think I'm that much of an amateur that I'd keep evidence relating to the thefts in my sock drawer.'

Lauren met the hooded threat in his eyes and panicked. She tried to move past him and was hauled back struggling as her wrists were captured and forced back against the wall.

The thin beach dress she wore over her bikini crept up her thighs as the enforced position put pressure on her clothes. His body menaced hers, and she turned her face to the side as he deliberately made her take his weight, his chest a hard wall against the soft upthrust of her breasts. She visibly flinched at the contact, unaware of the assessing gaze her flushed profile was being subjected to.

'That's what I thought.' Ryan's voice was even and he eased back, his thumb massaging one of her wrists in silent apology for her confinement. 'Tell me why making love frightens you, Lauren.'

Glaring at him through a wing of dark hair, Lauren tried to free her wrists to no avail. 'Making love? You don't know the meaning of the word. You're interested in sex, Ryan; let's not be afraid to use the word.'

'All right.' Ryan agreed reasonably. 'Why are you frightened of sex? Tell me or I'll kiss you until you do and I might just forget to stop.'

Ryan relaxed his body so that it brushed hers and a quiver of awareness racked her frame and was monitored mercilessly, the knowledge of her reaction in the mocking gleam of his eyes.

Lauren didn't trust him but believed he was capable of dragging a confession out of her. He surprised her with his curiosity. She had expected him to make the most of his advantage.

'Tell me.' This time there was an edge of restlessness in his voice and she stumbled into speech as his gaze touched on the gleaming copper of her thighs, exposed by the short dress.

'I was fostered as a child.' She bent her head, unwilling to share the rawness of her feelings on the matter. 'The father of the family was a little too friendly——' She heard him swear under his breath and closed her eyes as he released the pressure on her wrists and drew her to him. 'He didn't actually harm me. It was just the threat—— Anyway——' she brushed this aside '—I ran away—found Derek. He gave up university so that he could give me a home. He was only nineteen.' She impressed her brother's sense of responsibility on him.

'And it left you wary of men?' Ryan pursued the buried facts of the matter, his hand stroking over her hair comfortingly. She shuddered and his arms tightened. She had distracted him unwittingly from his original purpose. He was no longer concerned why she was in his cabin; he was intent on unravelling the mysteries of her past.

'So—you owe your brother a lot.' Ryan's voice made her lift her head.

'He has nothing to do with this, Ryan. He's innocent; this isn't misplaced loyalty——'

'You're the one who's been caught—twice,' he pointed out abrasively. 'My natural inclination is to lock you up and throw away the key. The trouble is,' his voice was loaded with self-mockery, 'I think I'd keep letting you out, just to convince myself I hadn't dreamt you.' The intense, absorbed expression on his face set off a subterranean chain reaction within Lauren. She was captivated by his gaze, and his voice caressed her, gently conquering the flimsy barriers of her defence.

'You're a rare thing, Lauren.' He watched his thumb brush against her jaw, his eyes narrowing on the moist pink quiver of her lips. 'You fascinate me.'

Bending his head, Ryan's breath feathered her lips. It needed only the slight upward movement of her head to seal the kiss. Lauren allowed the contact, wishing that he wouldn't confuse her with a pretence of caring. It made her vulnerable when she wanted to be strong. Facts were facts. He might offer a warm embrace and some semblance of comfort, but he made it plain where his interest truly lay. She fascinated him! He described her in terms of some collector's piece rather than anyone he found necessary to his existence. Ryan Daniels wouldn't know genuine emotion if it got up and bit him. Even his sister regarded him as an ambitious, cold-hearted automaton. Yet that computer chip he had for a heart was clothed in a deliciously deceptive cloak of masculinity that needed only the questing nuzzle of his lips against hers to make her criticism of his character dim to a brief whisper of caution.

It was that potent descent into sensuality he offered that didn't so much storm her long-maintained barriers but melted them away. The firm persuasion of his mouth made hers tremble and then cling, a rush of untrained emotions leaving her in helpless confusion.

Lauren had tied her hair into a plait that morning, leaving her nape exposed to his questing fingers, a quiver of feeling running through her as his caressing touch brought her pleasure. The thin black beach dress she wore, with a bright slash of colour running from the arm to the hem, moulded her body, the deep-cut neckline showing golden skin over the delicate collarbones, and descending to the rise of her breasts. A skimpy bikini was all she had on underneath. Pressing her to him, Ryan's hands pushed her dress up over her thighs, his mouth burning against hers, urging her to unleash her response. She trembled, unable to resist the onslaught of his caresses, incoherently whispering his name as he kissed a raging path down her throat to the golden curves of her breasts.

'Take this off,' Ryan demanded, easing back from her, his fingers sliding under the thin black strap at the shoulder and pushing it down her arm, then moving his palm back over her shoulder to stroke the naked area he had exposed. As he cupped her neck, the narrowing of her eyes in pleasure and the skittish shake of her head showed him his touch disturbed her.

'You don't kiss as if you're scared,' he murmured.

'I'm not——' The words were out before she could stop them, abruptly halted when he hooked his thumb under the remaining strap of her dress and pulled the material down, the scanty protection of her bikini making her feel as good as naked.

'Ryan...?'

'Making love can be as natural as breathing. There's nothing to be frightened of.' His voice soothed her protests as he drew her closer. The heat of his body engulfed her, the thin vest T-shirt he wore with shorts providing a transitory barrier to the hunger in their bodies. Lauren's breath shook in her throat as the hard demand of his masculine body inflamed the ache in her loins, her green eyes revealed dazed senses and her lips parted as Ryan's mouth covered hers purposefully.

The soft wash of the waves, the movement and subdued noise from the other inhabitants of the yacht faded as Lauren let her senses run free...free to the edge of wildness.

'Beautiful.' The word tickled her lips, and her lashes flickered open to meet the intensity of Ryan's gaze.

Lauren was having a hard time remembering why she was letting this man get so close. She was halfway to feeling—— It was stupid; she wanted to trust him, wanted so much to invite his strength into her life. The thought shocked her!

The sudden knock on the door was a jerk back to reality for both of them. Ryan swore under his breath, his eyes electric as they ran over the temptation before him. Making a brief gesture to her that suggested she tidy herself up, he moved to open the door. Lauren managed to retrieve the dress, which had fallen in a puddle on to the floor, and pulled it up, her hot cheeks and guilty expression revealing.

Penny stood outside and Ryan viewed her with feigned interest. 'There's a fire somewhere?' he prompted with heavy mockery.

'Lauren promised she would show me some of her designs.' Penny sounded over-bright, her dark eyes darting to Lauren's dazed features with the air of someone who felt they had arrived in the nick of time.

'Designs?' Ryan repeated as if his sister were addled.

'Yes, of course.' Lauren marshalled her reluctant limbs, meeting Ryan's eyes briefly with a measure of misgiving. It was not an escape, it was a postponement; that much Lauren could read easily.

'Phew.' Penny grinned at Lauren as they scuttled away from the cabin. 'Ryan wasn't amused. How did you explain being in his cabin?'

Lauren was reluctant to go into detail, her mind slow and sluggish, still in the grip of her senses.

'Is he pressurising you?' Penny was all sympathy. 'How despicable, using Derek to force you——'

'He doesn't do that.' Lauren preceded Ryan's sister into her cabin, her voice low but with protest underlying the denial. Penny's attention sharpened and Lauren felt and looked uncomfortable.

'Lauren, he's a wolf—I can't remember him having a caring relationship!'

'I said he doesn't force me.' Lauren resented the intrusion into her personal life. 'I didn't declare undying love.'

Penny Daniels viewed her with misgivings. 'He's quite capable of being behind all this. Don't let him hurt you, Lauren. If he finds out about Derek being on board, we'll both be in the firing line.'

Lauren shivered. Yes, she sensed that. Ryan responded to her vulnerability. If he suspected he had been manipulated, his pride would be dented, and male pride was unforgiving. She found it hard to believe he had orchestrated the robberies. On odd occasions he had been thoughtful. She couldn't believe he was thoroughly rotten.

'We're not getting very far, are we?' Penny couldn't hide her despondency. 'Poor Derek. How could anyone think he'd be dishonest?'

Lauren nodded, exchanging a sympathetic look with the other woman.

That night they reached the shores of Tortola and anchored in Brewer's Bay. It was decided that they would have a barbecue on the beach.

Tortola was the principal island of the British Virgin Islands. It still had a few rum distilleries functioning when the cane was harvested and, although it boasted Roadtown, the capital of the BVI, it had the same laid-back quality that marked many of the islands in the group. The lack of commercialism was deliberate, Lauren discovered from Lady Daniels. It seemed there was a genuine desire not to spoil the islands by allowing them to become the fun palaces of the West.

Brewer's Bay was isolated and reputedly romantic, and the best route to the beauty spot was by boat, although it was accessible by land. Knowing that there was to be a reckoning with Ryan, Lauren could have wished for somewhere a little less seductive.

She felt Ryan's presence before she turned her head to acknowledge him. He helped her into the launch that was to transport them to the remote beach; he had dispensed with the dinner-jacket and was dressed in khaki cotton trousers and a white shirt with pockets detailed on the breast.

'Did Penny buy anything?' he queried, his tone as blank as her expression. 'She was desperate to see your designs, as I remember.'

'Oh—yes, yes, she liked them.'

'Good.' His tone was dry.

Casting him a quick, apprehensive glance, Lauren discovered he was watching her and was glad when the roar of the small boat's outboard motor drowned any attempt at conversation. Her thigh-hugging denim shorts and shirt topped by a straw boater achieved a very female effect out of very masculine materials. She had felt like covering up, feeling defensive after the raw sexuality Ryan had drawn from her earlier that day.

It was impossible to avoid Ryan. They were, in the eyes of the others, a couple. He brought her a plate of food and a glass of wine, settling himself down beside her, the wind picking at his hair as he watched the surf crash on to the sand further down the beach. He didn't seem interested in eating; he hadn't chosen anything for himself, and Lauren found she couldn't summon up much of an appetite either.

Luc Rabanne produced a large, powerful ghetto-blaster and before long loud music polluted the peace of the night and Chantal was encouraging those around her to dance.

'Walk?' Ryan invited as Chantal got perilously close.

Lauren felt torn. If they left the others, it gave Ryan the chance to exert his sexual magnetism over her. If she stayed, he would doubtless punish her for disobedience and she favoured private humiliation to a more public version. Scrambling to her feet, she decided to face the inevitable and let him take her hand in his and fell into step with him as they moved away from the others with only the moon to guide them.

After a while, Lauren relaxed enough to slip her feet out of her sandals, tugging her hand free so that she could pick up her shoes. Ryan watched her as she let the surf wash over her toes. The moon was full, the sky purple under the silvery blaze.

'You haven't asked about your brother lately,' he commented, watching her stiffen and turn to look at him.

Lauren realised how that must look. Knowing Derek was on board the *Halcyon* had taken away the fear for his safety—at least from those thugs in London.

'Have you heard something?' She tried to inject the right amount of concern into her voice.

'No.' He was blunt. 'He appears to have disappeared without a trace. Very professional for an amateur.'

'Derek's innocent!' she maintained. 'He's probably frightened. How would you feel if someone planted incriminating evidence in your briefcase?'

'Is that what happened?' Ryan's voice silkily encouraged the train of thought.

'Derek never brought anything important home——'
Lauren halted, realising she was offering fresh excuses
backed up by what Derek had told her.

'So it was just a coincidence he phoned to ask you to
take the briefcase out?' Ryan came close as she waded
knee-deep in the water, creamy surf washing around his
shoes.

'It must have been.' She felt anxiety prickle over her
skin.

'You appear to have become very friendly with Penny.
If I were the sensitive type, I might suspect a con-
spiracy,' he said.

How could she ever imagine Ryan Daniels could be
taken in? He might not have all the details but his brain
was quickly assembling all the facts at his disposal.

'I was as surprised as you were when she——' Lauren
faltered, realising she could easily lead him to believe
she had not welcomed the intrusion.

'Interrupted us.' Ryan was suspiciously helpful. 'Yes,
that was probably genuine. You weren't expecting to lose
yourself like that.'

Lauren evaded his scrutiny, turning her head to gaze
out to sea. Lose herself? Yes, she could easily do that.
She flirted with the danger he represented even now; she
couldn't manufacture the indignation to flounce away
from him and rejoin the others. Snatches of music drifted
towards them, the rhythms of the islands joyful, infinitely sensual. Between them, the silence grew, the
tension growing by the second.

'What do you want?' She turned to face him, unable
to bear it any longer. 'Some kind of admission of guilt?
Yes, I'm friendly with Penny. You're right; she disturbed us on purpose. She told me you've never cared
for anyone. Your own sister thinks you're driven by cold-
hearted ambition and use people to serve your own

purpose.' She moved to pass him, strong emotion marking her features as he caught her and hauled her round. 'Unlike you——' she tried to prise his fingers from her wrist '—I do have feelings. I don't intend to put myself at your me-ercy.' His grip remained immovable.

Ryan's eyes narrowed angrily, his lean face taut with anger. He considered himself fireproof and he'd been called a lot worse, but discovering his sister protecting Lauren from his exploitation touched a nerve.

'You are at my mercy,' his voice lashed at her. 'I could throw you to the wolves. Those documents being in your possession is all I need to ruin you and your precious brother. Fortunately for you, I have more interest in the truth than seeing you in court.'

'Purely altruistic, of course,' she accused him mockingly. 'You wouldn't be interested in getting me into bed, would you?'

'Beautiful women aren't scarce.' His tone was clipped. 'Cold-hearted ambition doesn't leave room for obsessive lust, Lauren. To accuse me of one you'll have to modify the other.'

'Why should I bother? Neither are admirable attributes.' She glared at him, desperately fuelling her chaotic emotions to withstand him.

Ryan's chest heaved as he glowered down at her but slowly he mastered the fury within him, regaining some agility of thought.

'You camouflage well, Lauren.' His hands tightened on her, pulling her closer. 'You must be learning to get under my skin. It's not like me to miss the signs but I'm not used to inexperienced women.'

'You're detestable!'

'I'm a fool.'

'Ryan——' She tried to pull back.

'Shut up, Lauren,' he breathed against her mouth, cutting off her protest, his tongue audaciously stroking between the parted pearls of her teeth.

'Don't.' The whisper held little conviction; her mouth was already relaxed for his persuasion as he deepened the kiss, spinning Lauren's senses madly into communion with the surf on the beach, the distant calypso music and the lift and fall of palm trees.

She had been in her tight little prison too long. Her senses were starved, welcoming the rousing stroke of his hands. His fingers curved over her hips, sweeping down to her thighs, pulling her against him, letting her become accustomed to the intimate fit of their bodies.

Gathering the dark river of her hair into his hands, Ryan kissed her fluttering eyelids, his teeth grazing her cheekbones as if he wanted to taste her like some ripe fruit. The swollen pinkness of her mouth he nipped and nuzzled until it opened like a flower giving up its honey. The groan in his throat reverberated through her. She felt like that—relieved and tortured at the same time. Her tongue moved in a love dance against his, her thighs hurting from the ache of wanting.

Clutching at his shoulders for support, Lauren found herself lifted up against him into his arms and carried to a place of shadow under the palm trees. Placing her back on her feet, Ryan held her gaze while he undid the fastenings on his shirt, exposing the smooth gold musculature that had tormented her when lying beside him on the sun-lounger. Spreading the shirt out on the sand, he came back to her, the warmth of his skin making her reach out to touch him. Capturing her hands, he held them against his throat and urged her to stroke over his chest, his silvery gaze possessing hers as her thumbs brushed against the line of dark hair disappearing beneath the waistband of his trousers. The shock of what she wanted showed on her face and Ryan cradled her against him, stroking her hair, whispering words of reassurance between kisses.

When he pulled at the studs on the shirt she wore, Lauren stiffened, but the heat of him drew her pale body and she pressed herself against him as he drew the denim back over her shoulders. She had a model's body. Small, pert breasts, a long back, slender waist, slim hips, flat stomach, fragile without any surplus flesh. Ryan's hands moved over her as if fashioning a new creation.

His voice purred over her senses. 'You haunt my fantasies, Lauren. It's getting so bad, I can't think of anything else.'

Lauren returned his kiss with a feeling of deep inevitability. She felt like that too—drawn to a flame, primitive and beyond understanding. Burying her fingers into his hair, Lauren watched his mouth move moistly over her upper chest. The dark tip of her breast felt dry and sore. She closed her eyes in ecstasy, letting her head fall back as he kissed and then consumed the erect peak. The world became crazy. Lauren lost balance and found herself guided to the cotton shirt that protected her from the sand.

The moon gilded high in the sky, filling Lauren's vision with silver brilliance. It seemed to blank out all thought. She felt the zip fastening her shorts give, and swallowed drily. Ryan's hand on her ribcage slid down over her stomach, his thumb brushing below her navel. She looked a picture of female abandon, her dark hair tangled around her shoulders, the denim shirt halfway down her arms, her shorts loosened to show the angle of her hip and plane of her stomach. Ryan Daniels had never met a woman who presented him with such a mixture of images. The way she looked enticed him to take her without thought for anything but his own release. But, if he accepted the story she had handed him she was probably a virgin and trembled because she was frightened.

'Lauren?' He brushed her lips with his, his fingers pushing aside the denim and cupping the delicate female mound covered with a thin strip of silk.

Closing her eyes, Lauren folded her arms around his neck, her mouth searching for his, shudders of desire shaking her body as Ryan introduced her to the fire in her own body and burnt her up in the conflagration. She felt his movements as he divested them both of their remaining clothes, felt his warmth as he covered her body with his.

Wanting her so badly, Ryan couldn't believe he possessed such depths of restraint. Gently, he moved against her, testing the delicate well of her womanhood, the tight sheath closing around him until he could deny himself no longer and he surged against her, hearing her cry of pain.

'It's over,' he comforted her finally, placing small kisses around her mouth. 'I won't hurt you like that again, sweetheart.'

Lauren felt the pain ebb away to leave the new sensation of their coupling, and Ryan's mouth took hers in heated demand, his restlessness the edge of a growing storm as he accustomed her to the demands of his body.

When it happened she couldn't tell but it felt as if the moon had settled its brilliance in a tight coin of light in her loins, the burn making her twist and strain to be free of it. Ryan seemed to pour his strength into making the silver fire glow and glitter, every thrust of his body making the light blaze brighter until her nails scratched him wildly to be free.

Catching her wrists, Ryan pushed them above her head, riding the storm in the woman, seeking the heat in her loins with instinctive need to be deep within her. Suddenly the brilliance exploded and Lauren cried out, the primitive keening absorbed in the crash of the surf, music only for the man possessing her.

She remained in a dream state for some time after they made love, allowing Ryan to wash her in the surf and help her with her clothes. Taking the lapels of her shirt between his fingers, Ryan pressed a hard kiss against her mouth.

'I'm glad you can be honest about something.' He shook his head, and his mouth curled indulgently as he fastened the studs and stroked her hair back into some semblance of order. 'Come on, dream child, it's time we got back.'

Lauren sheltered in the curve of Ryan's arm as the boat took them back to the yacht, allowing his leisurely possession of her mouth whenever he chose to indulge himself.

Later, when she lay in her cabin, waves of mortification made her groan out loud and bury her face into the pillow. How could she have allowed Ryan Daniels so close? She had complicated things unbearably. It was all going to explode in her face. What had started as a convenient charade now had all the trappings of truth. Ryan wanted her. Now they had made love she had the feeling dark tides were moving her into dangerous seas of emotion. Ryan resented his ordered world being thrown into confusion by anything as elemental as—what had he called it?—'obsessive lust.' If he could find a way of limiting the damage she had done to his life, she was convinced he would do it! And along with that certainty came another: Ryan Daniels could hurt her more than any other living being and why that was so she refused to contemplate.

CHAPTER FIVE

LAUREN awoke the next morning to a gentle rap on the door. Peering at her watch, she noted she had missed breakfast and she assumed a tray was being delivered. Shouting, 'Come in,' she disappeared into the bathroom.

After a quick shower, she pulled on her bathrobe and was rubbing a towel around her neck when she caught sight of Ryan lounging on her bed, drinking tea from one of the two cups that had been served on the tray.

'What are you doing?' she demanded indignantly.

'Surprisingly enough, I missed breakfast too.' He viewed her leisurely. 'How do you feel this morning? You look as if you've lost your virginity and rediscovered your temper.'

'Everyone will think we've spent the night together!' She viewed the tray with horror.

'Isn't that what people are supposed to think?' he queried, sounding amused.

'No. I mean, I know I'm supposed to be your girl-friend but——'

'I'm afraid the two things are synonymous. I don't go in for platonic relationships.'

'I didn't think you went in for relationships,' she whipped back at him, her green eyes militant.

'I don't as a rule. I don't have time. But you're the exception—I've even taken you home to meet Mother.' He grinned at his own humour. 'Tea?'

'It would choke me.' She glared at him, her mind working feverishly. What worried her was not so much what her fellow travellers thought of her—they wouldn't

turn a hair—but the fact that the staff would know that
Ryan was breakfasting with her meant Derek would too.
He knew she had never had a serious boyfriend, and
heaven knew what he'd make of her apparent closeness
to Ryan. Penny's view that she was being blackmailed
into a sexual relationship might prompt him into doing
something stupid.

'What would you like to do today? We should reach
St John's within the next hour; it's hardly a great
metropolis but it has some beautiful beaches,' he said.

'I don't know; I haven't decided yet. Do you mind
leaving while I get dressed?' she asked.

'Yes, I mind very much.' He regarded her steadily. 'I
don't like women who sulk, so tell me what's wrong.'

Where did she begin? Everything was wrong. Even if
there hadn't been the robbery, she wouldn't have chosen
a high-powered executive with a recreational attitude to
sex as her first lover.

'Last night was a mistake,' she blazed at him. 'Don't
expect me to indulge in a casual affair just because——' Words failed her.

'Just because you couldn't get enough of me last
night?' he supplied helpfully, getting to his feet.

'Lauren?' Penny's voice came from outside. 'Can I
come in?'

'No!' Ryan answered for her, moving to block off the
door.

Lauren tried to push past him and he caught the belt
of her gown, pulling her to him, his light eyes blazing
down into hers.

'Tell her she's redundant as a chaperon—I've already
had you.'

'Get out,' she spat at him, 'before I scream the place
down!'

Ryan very effectively put his hand over her mouth and smiled nastily as she tried to bite him. 'I'll call back for you in an hour. You're obviously not at your best first thing.'

'I hate you,' she screamed impotently, stamping her foot as the door closed behind him.

She searched the *Halcyon* for Derek, but when she came across Penny Daniels she discovered he had gone in the boat with the first party departing for Caneel Bay.

'Ryan's in a really bad mood,' Penny commented curiously, openly admiring Lauren's scarlet beach dress, which was raffishly matched with her straw boater, which also had a ribbon to match. 'Have you had a row?'

'You could say that.' Lauren pushed a hand through her fringe, dislodging the boater and having to replace it as it slipped backwards. 'Have you seen Derek this morning? Did he say anything to you?'

Penny lowered her lashes. 'He's worried about you. You know how men are. Luc Rabanne was teasing Ryan about disappearing from the beach party—Derek overheard.'

Lauren felt her blood beat a path to her cheeks. 'And what did Ryan say?' she muttered, temporarily distracted.

'Something slick and non-committal. Ryan doesn't need to prove himself, does he?' Penny's eyes moved behind her. 'Talk of the devil.'

Lauren stiffened as Ryan joined them with Richard Harrington in tow. It seemed the two men had decided to hire a jeep and drive around the island. The sea views alone were supposed to be wonderful, and Lauren acquiesced, considering the company of the other couple an improvement on being alone with Ryan. The situation was beginning to stifle her. If she openly went to war with him, not only would the cruise be uncomfortable but Derek would forget his own concerns and come to her rescue. The only alternative was to be ruthlessly manipulated by Ryan and, despite her antipathy, she didn't doubt where that would lead.

Ryan opted to drive and Lauren took the passenger-seat beside him. Despite the turmoil of emotions within, the beauty of the sleepy island worked its magic. St John was one of the islands that came under the auspices of the United States.

'Most of the island is National Park,' Ryan informed her. 'The population amounts to a few thousand. It's remarkably unspoilt.'

Meeting his eyes, Lauren realised he was having a dig at her for her petulant attitude that morning. She had been 'unspoilt' until he got his marauding hands on her; now she felt as if every nerve was frighteningly alive and she would never be free of the hunger he had sown in her body.

They stopped off in Trunk Bay, Ryan and Richard leaving the two girls to explore the snorkelling trail, an underwater park for the less experienced divers. They went on to the end of the beach where the coral reputedly provided a wonderland of colour.

On the way back, they picnicked near a clump of kapok trees overlooking a small emerald-fringed bay of white sand and sweeping surf.

Lauren was unpacking the hamper when Richard Harrington joined her. He helped her unfold the small picnic chairs and then showed her a leaf he had picked from a nearby tree. Rubbing it between his finger and thumb, he stroked his finger lightly across her throat.

'Recognise that?'

Lauren didn't much like Richard Harrington but she tried not to show it. 'It's familiar. It smells like rum.'

'They make St John's Bay Rum cologne out of it. It's a bay-leaf.'

Taking the leaf he proffered, she sniffed at it and then looked up to where Ryan stood with Penny viewing the bay below. He switched his gaze to his sister but not before she received the impression he had been watching her. A tremor of feeling ran through her. She felt branded, driven down a shadowed path to a future she couldn't see and had little part in choosing.

'Never play Ryan at chess.' Richard Harrington seemed aware of her thoughts.

She met his eyes and found only playful friendship there. 'I don't play chess,' she replied lightly, but the impression that she had been warned stayed with her.

After a leisurely lunch, they continued their circuit of the island. The roads weren't paved and Lauren winced as they bumped their way towards Cruz Bay, St John's capital.

'Couldn't you just stay here forever?' Penny shouted above the engine to her.

Lauren couldn't deny the islands had their attraction but situated as they were between the Caribbean and the Atlantic Ocean she found the concept of a scatter of islands amid great bodies of water rather intimidating.

'I think I'd need to have a boat,' she responded. 'The isolation might prove too much.'

'There's always the *Goose*,' Ryan informed her, smiling at her puzzled look. 'It runs between here and St Croix.' Glancing at his watch, he nodded. 'We should make the return trip. What about you, Penny? Do you want to see the islands by air?'

'No, thanks.' Penny sounded diffident. 'I hope you've got a strong stomach, Lauren.'

Ryan laughed, shaking his head, his silver-blue eyes alive with good humour as they met the query in

Lauren's. 'It really isn't that bad. The *Goose* is a seaplane. It's the Caribbean bus service.'

Lauren digested this. It didn't sound as if they'd be alone too much, not enough for any in-depth conversation to put her back on the spot, anyway.

'It sounds fun.' She smiled back, wishing Ryan's good mood didn't double his attraction. He looked as much at home in the brightly coloured vest and shorts as he did in formal wear. To have that coloured hair and tan as well made him look golden and, she reluctantly added, delicious. Lauren's body suffered a momentary pang of weakness before a severe jolt reminded her to cling firmly on to the door. Whatever the *Goose* entailed it couldn't be worse than travelling by road, she decided.

Saying goodbye to Penny and Richard Harrington, she surveyed their new form of transport dubiously.

'Does it actually work?' she asked, earning grins from some of the waiting passengers.

'Have faith.' Ryan waved her on to the plane. 'I've arranged for you to have the co-pilot's seat. It gives the best view.'

'What about the co-pilot?' she muttered, only to find herself at the receiving end of several amused grins once more. 'Don't tell me—there isn't a co-pilot.' She bore it stoically, assured that if Ryan was willing to trust this peculiar cross between a boat and plane then it wouldn't dare fall out of the sky—that was if it ever got into the air!

Strapping herself in, she couldn't help a hasty glance at the pilot as the *Goose* lurched down the ramp towards the choppy blue water. She was not a bit reassured when he cranked up the undercarriage by hand.

'Good grief.' Water splashed up as the sea-plane took off and defeated the physical laws Lauren had been taught at school by getting airborne. Hearty chuckles

from behind suggested her response had been overheard
and her reactions eagerly awaited, but as soon as the
horror of take-off had worn off she discovered it was a
wonderful way to view the islands.

St Thomas, Tortola, Virgin Gorda were emeralds en-
crusted with diamond shores in a sapphire sea. Where
else could such purity of colour be found bathed in a
climate that truly suggested paradise? No wonder the
breathless hush broken only by swaying trees and the
chatter of birds held sway over the distant Virgin Islands.
The population, she decided, must be in a constant state
of wonder.

'Impressed?' Ryan's voice came from behind her. She
turned, her eyes reflecting her delight.

'It's wonderful. Thank you for bringing me,' she said.

He merely smiled and Lauren turned back to immerse
herself in the beauty of it all, something telling her that
Ryan had decided to relax the pressure on her, probably
considering her odd behaviour evoked by the emotional
upheaval caused by their lovemaking.

They didn't have much time to spend on St Croix,
landing in the capital Christiansted and just glimpsing
the charming waterfront before finding a charter to take
them back to the *Halcyon*.

'We'll be docking in St Croix in the next day or two,'
Ryan explained his reluctance to linger there for any
length of time.

The journey back was no less spectacular. Lauren sat
on the small deck, watching the silvery trail of water left
by the boat as it ploughed the sun-glittered sea. The
mixture of colour reminded her of Ryan's eyes. She
pinched her arm to punish herself for dwelling on such
things. She must quell the attraction she felt for him,
not feed it.

Ryan had taken the opportunity to use the time to try his hand at hooking one of the big fish known to run off the coast of St Croix. Lauren had heard the men talking of blue marlin, sharks and wahoo that were hunted as much for the challenge as the food value of the catch. The blue marlin, she knew, were the prize of the game fish and would fight for hours before they were captured or escaped.

Predictably enough, Ryan had his tussle with a 'white'—a white marlin, not as big but sometimes trickier, the grizzled West Indian captain informed her, shouting encouragement at Ryan while his grandson, a skinny eight-year-old, gave the benefit of his knowledge, his feet barely staying on the deck in the excitement.

I'm like that fish, Lauren thought, watching the battle as Ryan alternatively let the white run and then reeled in again. Game—she was brutal with herself—hunted in the seas and islands of the Caribbean for no other purpose than the challenge. The only difference was that the marlin was putting up a better fight!

She nearly cheered when the line snapped, and was surprised to see Ryan laugh. Probably public school training, she reflected sourly. Not whether you win or lose, but how you play the game. She couldn't imagine him losing quite so gracefully with her.

Lauren was given a glass of chilled lime juice, while Ryan, she observed, was provided with a can of beer and appeared to be exchanging stories with their captain. Lauren hated to admit it but she became rather piqued by his lack of interest. It was one thing to give her breathing space, quite another to leave her to her own devices for hours. Her mind reluctantly dragged itself away from Ryan and instead pondered her present predicament. No doubt by the time they got back to the *Halcyon* Penny Daniels would have regaled Derek with the fact that Ryan had been in her cabin that morning and, when this was added to Luc Rabanne's remarks, she would have the pair of them interrogating her.

'Not far now.' Ryan came to join her some time later, absorbing the hint of resentment she couldn't disguise. 'What's the matter? Got over the sulks and want some attention?' he responded, to her dissatisfaction.

Giving him a killing look, she was unable to gauge his response—his eyes were shielded by dark sunglasses.

'I do not sulk!'

'You do a very good impression.' Smiling knowingly, he laughed low in his throat. 'You were really rooting for that fish, weren't you?'

'It gave me hope.' She pretended to take an interest in a sea-bird shadowing the boat, wondering why she felt miserable now the wonder of the flight on the sea-plane was behind them. 'It's nice to know escape is possible,' she added.

'Not for you,' he muttered drily, drawing a quick glance from his companion. 'There's a fever in your blood, Lauren. Without me, it would burn you up.'

'You don't fool me,' she denied his assertion hotly. 'I could say goodbye and leave you without a single regret. And as soon as this is over I'll do exactly that.'

He didn't bother denying her words, but Lauren didn't feel she'd won her point.

On returning to the boat, she showered and after drying her hair lay on the bed flicking through some fashion magazines she had bought in Antigua. She must have dozed off to be woken with a start when Penny shook her and called her name.

'He's done what?' Lauren peered at her through a haze of sleep, consciousness returning rapidly as she took in the news. 'He must have lost his senses.' Derek, it tran-spired, had decided to face Ryan Daniels. 'Couldn't he have waited until we finished the cruise?' Knowing there was nowhere to run made her get up and move about agitatedly.

'Derek was angry. He——' Penny caught the flash of Lauren's green eyes and quailed. 'He doesn't approve of the way—er—Ryan's been treating you.'

'*He* doesn't!' Lauren's incredulous expression made the other girl move uncomfortably. Was he under the illusion it would get any better when Ryan knew they had conspired to deceive him?

Penny looked glum. 'I thought you wanted to tell Ryan. I mean, he's far more capable of sorting out the situation than we are; he knows the right people.'

Lauren's brows drew together in consternation. 'I thought Ryan was a suspect.'

'We panicked a bit.' Penny was rueful. 'I suppose we imagined ourselves in some Agatha Christie drama, where all the clues would be there to find. It's not like that, is it? I mean, he is my brother. He dislikes Richard but I don't think he'd deliberately hurt me.'

She was fortunate. Lauren hugged her arms around her body. She had the feeling any retribution was going to find its way to *her* door.

'He can't make you stay with him, Lauren.' Penny sounded doubtful. 'Can he?'

That rather depended on what he decided to do with the evidence against Derek and herself. He had a witness to prove she had tried to take information out of the building. Unable to sit and await her fate, Lauren went to the door.

'Don't you think we should give Derek moral support?' she asked.

Penny didn't look over-enthusiastic but followed her co-conspirator out of the room.

The sound of raised voices made them cringe as they approached Ryan's cabin, and the thud that followed made them forget courtesy and burst in to find Ryan stroking his jaw and Derek sprawled on the floor.

'Ah, the ladies.' Ryan's eyes were as grey and stormy as pewter skies. 'Tell your brother I didn't rape you, Lauren, before I'm forced to knock him senseless.'

'You bastard——' Derek launched himself at his adversary, who caught him and drew back his fist to find Lauren hanging on his arm and Penny attempting to pull Derek away.

'Derek, what are you doing?' Lauren ignored Ryan's growled instruction to get out of the way.

'I'm going to teach Mr High and Mighty a lesson. We may not be wealthy, Lauren, but we don't have to use moral blackmail to get what we want out of life.'

'And I do, I suppose.' Ryan's voice was cold and flinty.

'Why else would my sister have anything to do with you? I'd rather go to prison than have her in your clutches——'

'That can be arranged,' Ryan grated, casting a glance at Lauren, who had blushed bright red.

'Embarrassed, Lauren? You surprise me. Perhaps we could bring an end to this pantomime.' He gave Derek's hair a critical look. 'You're too late to save your sister's virtue, Walsh, but if it's any comfort she's going to become my wife as soon as I can arrange it.'

Derek looked astonished, his questioning glance at Lauren avoided as she averted her eyes.

'Aren't you, darling?' Ryan persisted.

Lauren searched his harsh, unrelenting features, thinking quickly. 'I haven't promised anything yet, Ryan.' Her voice was husky. 'And I don't think this is an appropriate time for announcements of any kind.' Reaching up, she touched his bruised jaw with manufactured concern. She had to give herself time. If she let Derek see she was antagonistic to Ryan, he would continue on this self-destructive crusade to avenge the wrong he felt had been done to her.

Ryan's eyes glittered with triumph. 'Perhaps now we can sort this mess out.' He placed his arm around Lauren's shoulders, satisfied that she understood his unspoken terms.

He listened while Derek and Penny revealed their story, his mouth thinning occasionally with impatience. Lauren sat beside him, perfectly aware that her fate would be decided separately and, she feared, at much greater cost.

'So apparently you were the one who was supposed to take the briefcase out, not Lauren? It was just coincidence that you forgot your briefcase and Lauren provided the thieves with a much more distracting courier?' Ryan questioned.

'Yes.' Derek was uncomfortable with Ryan Daniels's manner of observing his sister, but as she didn't protest it was hard to make an objection.

'And you were in Paris when the briefcase was in Lauren's possession?'

'Yes. I flew over on Friday morning.'

'So why have you evaded my attempts to question you? The evidence against you is purely circumstantial.'

Derek shared a look with Penny and she answered for him.

'We thought someone might want Derek incriminated. Richard would lose out if the engagement was broken——'

'And I would gain the presidency?' Ryan finished the equation coolly. 'I think you overestimate Harrington's challenge.' He looked thoughtful. 'For the sake of the atmosphere on board I suggest you disembark at St Thomas. Penny can sort out the complications in her love life and you can get back to work.' Turning his head, he brushed his lips over Lauren's temple. 'Does that sound all right to you, darling?'

'Yes.' She felt the full weight of the word settle heavily on her shoulders. She owed Derek such a lot—she would rather face Ryan on her own than let him destroy her brother.

The cabin door closed behind Derek and Penny and for endless seconds the only sound came from the slow, rhythmical whir of the fan and the subdued lap of the sea against the hull.

' "And then there was one".' Ryan's voice was like the soft patter of rain before a storm—she could hear the low growl of thunder in the distance. 'You appear to be the only one caught red-handed without any mitigating circumstances,' he remarked.

'Spare me the courtroom drama——' she began.

'I won't spare you a damn thing!' He made her jump with shock, her face tense at the condemnation in his eyes. 'I don't enjoy being played for a fool! I've shielded you from the courts and from the thugs who broke into your flat.' Anger vibrated through him, his eyes blazing. 'Is that why you let me make love to you—some last-ditch attempt to make things easy for yourself?'

Lauren quivered, wounded yet still proud. 'I didn't let you, Ryan, I just didn't stop you. You'll be telling me I seduced you next.'

Laying a finger against her lips, Ryan grated, 'Enough,' with barely restrained force. 'If it hadn't been your first time, I would believe anything.'

Lauren felt as if every bone in her body weighed a ton, and when Ryan seized her shoulders she was too weary to make more than a token effort to pull away.

He searched her features for signs of deceit. 'How long have you known your brother was on board *Halcyon*?

From the beginning? Did you know he was in Paris with Penny?'

'No!' she disclaimed hotly. 'I didn't know where he was.'

'You knew yesterday when I caught you in my cabin. You knew last night but you lied when I brought the subject up. Why do you expect me to believe you're telling the truth now?'

Lauren looked up into his accusing face with a feeling of defeat. 'What's the point in this, Ryan? You don't want to believe me. You just want me to admit I'm guilty and I won't!'

Regarding the proud tilt of her head and the fervency of her self-belief, Ryan expelled his breath heavily, exasperated with the situation and exasperated with her.

'You could sell ice to Eskimos,' he growled, his hands falling away from her shoulders; he moved away from her, prowling the room, leaving her to watch him nervously.

The silence unnerved her; he was thinking deeply and she was too rattled to await her fate passively. 'Why did you tell Derek we were getting married? I thought the situation was complicated enough,' she said.

'No, it gets very simple from now on.' Ryan stopped, leaning back against the cabin door, effectively trapping her. 'You play things my way. You either marry me or seek justice through the courts. My board of directors want someone's head for those breaches of security. I either offer yours or continue my investigations elsewhere.'

'You'd prosecute me?' She couldn't believe he could be so callous.

'It's a straightforward deal. You need protecting and I need a wife. You trusted me with your body,' he reminded her, his gaze glazing with remembered intimacy.

GET 4 BOOKS
A CUDDLY TEDDY
AND A MYSTERY GIFT

Return this card, and we'll send you 4 Mills & Boon Romances, absolutely FREE! We'll even pay the postage and packing for you!

We're making you this offer to introduce you to the benefits of Mills & Boon Reader Service: free home delivery of brand-new Romance novels, at least a month before they're available in the shops, FREE gifts and a monthly Newsletter packed with offers and information.

Accepting these 4 free books places you under no obligation to buy, you may cancel at any time, even just after receiving your free shipment.

Yes, please send me 4 free Mills & Boon Romances, a Cuddly Teddy and a Mystery Gift as explained above. Please also reserve a Reader Service Subscription for me. If I decide to subscribe, I shall receive six superb new titles every month for just £10.20 postage & packing free. If I decide not to subscribe I shall write to you within 10 days. The free books and gifts will be mine to keep in any case. I understand that I am under no obligation whatsoever. I may cancel or suspend my subscription at any time simply by writing to you.

Ms/Mrs/Miss/Mr _____ 4A3R

Address _____

_____ Postcode_____

Signature_____
I am over 18 years of age.

Get 4 Books a Cuddly Teddy and Mystery Gift FREE!

SEE BACK OF CARD FOR DETAILS

Mills & Boon Reader Service,
FREEPOST
P.O. Box 236
Croydon
CR9 9EL

MPS
MAILING PREFERENCE SERVICE

No stamp needed

'Caribbean madness,' she retaliated, her face suffusing with colour. 'My trust was certainly misplaced.'

'I don't remember letting you down.' Ryan's silvery gaze returned to her face, taking in the play of emotions she was unable to disguise.

'I don't think we're talking about the same thing!'

He laughed, a strangely warm sound in the harsh battle of wits between them.

'You know I'm innocent!' she protested. 'You must feel that deep down or you wouldn't have helped me the way you have.'

'I know nothing of the sort,' Ryan corrected her brutally. 'Finding out you were a thief didn't stop me wanting you. I don't feel very good about that but——' He shrugged, his attitude one of self-derision. 'Just thank your lucky stars you have an unforgettable face.'

The last thing Lauren felt was lucky! She had been framed, robbed and was now being bludgeoned into marriage.

'We'll get married as soon as I can arrange it. We can stay on one of the islands for a couple of days for our honeymoon; that way it won't be blatantly obvious when I keep you in bed,' he told her.

Lauren blushed hotly, wishing the idea didn't send shivers of anticipation through her body and she could put up a convincing protest.

'Well?' he asked softly, taking hold of the lapels of her shirt and tugging slightly so that she swayed near to him. 'Give me your answer.'

Lauren felt his desire to trap and possess her entwine her with invisible bonds. Ryan Daniels needed to control the wild card she represented in his life, bringing his emotional life back into the realms of safety. It doomed any tenderness in their relationship and she felt the loss of something she had barely recognised with a sudden pang of agony.

Closing her eyes to shut him out, feeling his warm breath on her face, she dared not call his bluff. The implications were clear. Ryan might cite her as the only visible culprit but her brother wouldn't escape the smear of any investigation. His job would be on the line and, if Daniels and Blackthorn fired him, who else would consider him for employment? His relationship with Penny would be forfeited. She knew her brother would never allow the young woman to tie herself to a man without a future. She couldn't allow Derek to walk into the firing line as soon as he disembarked at Heathrow. Their young lives had been darkened by tragedy, but now at least one of them held the seeds of happiness within his grasp—she couldn't deny her brother his future.

'Lauren?'

'Yes!' Her lashes parted and she turned her face away angrily as he would have kissed her. 'As this is blackmail, I don't think we should cloud the issue with false sentiment.' She tried to free her lapels from his grasp.

'Very well.' He released her, his mouth depressing in regret but his eyes mocking her. 'There's an art to giving in gracefully, Lauren; I'll take great pleasure in teaching you.'

'You may find I'm a slow learner.' Lauren turned to the door, flicking him a rebellious glance.

His smile widened but the threat remained. 'We'll see. And Lauren——' She paused, wondering what was to come. 'Let's keep our arrangement just between the two of us.'

With a slight nod, she escaped.

CHAPTER SIX

A TROPICAL wedding on the island of St Croix sounded like a dream come true. Ryan Daniels slid the gold wedding-band on to Lauren's finger, the bride dressed in one of her own designs made by Cruzan seamstresses working throughout the night. The dress had gone some way to convincing her brother she was serious about loving Ryan. She had worked on its creation with all the dedication of an eager bride, getting through the charade by secretly pretending it was meant for someone else.

Penny acted as Lauren's bridesmaid, despite her misgivings on the haste and Derek's lingering doubts about the match. Derek had been dispatched home with the cool ruthlessness that was clearly evident when Ryan wanted to achieve some goal.

They were to honeymoon on St Croix, their hotel overlooking the harbour at Christiansted, while the others travelled on to St Kitts.

Lauren was glad to be free of the need to socialise and pretend to be deliriously happy even if the cessation of celebrations meant she was alone with Ryan.

'What do you think of Christiansted?' He pushed at the slatted doors, opening them out on to the balcony to reveal a view of blue sea and the rise and dip of masts, the tinkle of the rigging like wind chimes on the breeze.

'It's very beautiful.' She joined him, drinking in the colours and scents of the island paradise.

'So are you,' he murmured close to her ear, his arm sliding around her waist and bringing her into the curve of his body.

Lauren felt uncomfortably hot, her pulse beating an urgent tattoo when he unpinned her head-dress and let the dark river of her hair free from its bonds.

'Sometimes...' his voice was reflective as he arranged her hair over her shoulders, viewing the results with lazy satisfaction '...I wonder if you're worth the trouble you cause me.'

Lauren's eyes glinted with an emerald fire totally distinct from passion. 'Forgive me if I don't sympathise.' She tossed her hair back as if denying his right to window-dress her for his own pleasure.

Ryan smiled, viewing the virginal lace and purity of the wedding dress. 'Give in, Lauren. It's a waste of energy to fight.' Lean fingers stroked the line of her neck, discovering the hectic race of her blood beneath the silk of her skin. The intimate understanding in his gaze made Lauren's knees quake. 'You have all the qualities of unexploded dynamite. Before I took you, you were sending out sparks, singeing every man on board the yacht. You can't handle the way you feel. You can't control any of it without me to help you.' His voice held her in its spell as his fingers stroked over the bodice of her dress and undid the small pearl buttons fastening the delicate material. 'For my sins, you intrigue me. If I had to design my perfect woman...' he paused as his hand pushed aside the silk to reveal the lacy teddy she wore underneath '...she would look and feel like you.'

Stroking the lacy cup away from her breast, he explored the round curve of her shoulder and the delicate sculpture of bone and flesh. 'I think I have enough experience to cope with your emotional vandalism.' He let his finger stroke under her chin and tilted her face up, aware of the resentment in the depths of her eyes. 'I'll let you grow up, repair the damage that man in your past did to you, and my price is simply—pleasure.' His mouth closed on hers, feeling her lips tremble with the struggle of her emotions. Tantalisingly, he played with the soft, velvety texture of her mouth, tasting her, biting her gently until he felt the heave of her breasts against his chest and the small choked cry signalling her submission.

The phone ringing in the reception area of the suite made Ryan tear his lips from Lauren's in exasperated protest.

'Brilliant timing,' he muttered, his eyes moving restlessly over her face, dropping to where the unfastened bodice had fallen open, revealing the shadow of her cleavage. The mixture of lace and ivory satin against her skin drew his touch and then as it became clear that whoever wished to contact him was not about to give up he released her. 'I won't be long,' he grated, and from his tone Lauren gathered the person on the other end of the line wasn't likely to get a friendly reception.

Putting her hands up to her hot cheeks, she was shattered by the mixture of relief and mind-numbing regret. What was she doing, passively allowing him to unwrap her like some overdue Christmas present? She might be stuck with this marriage but that didn't mean she had to make it easy for him. If he wanted her to be a siren in bed and 'suitable' during the day, he had another think coming!

Peering between her fingers, her eyes alighted on a wardrobe and she rushed across the room, flinging it open. Dragging out a floral skirt and matching top, she hastily divested herself of her wedding gown and, grabbing some sandals, made for the balcony. Cruzan buildings were generally no more than a couple of storeys high due to the violent weather sometimes experienced, and she jumped down on to the sloping roof below and shinned down a convenient palm tree. Feeling as if she'd escaped from prison, she ignored the curious looks that witnessed her unusual exit from the hotel and mingled with the crowd, imagining Ryan's surprise with unmitigated glee.

Later, however, when the night darkened and she realised she had no money, her glee changed to disquiet. She couldn't meekly go back. It occurred to her that this time she would find it hard to deflect Ryan's anger. She had exhausted her supply of diversionary tactics. Tears might help but she had the feeling her new husband was smart enough to discern the crocodile variety. It was a temporary relief to stumble across the last-night celebration of a group of Americans. One of them recognised her from a perfume commercial she had done and she was soon supplied with a plateful of food and a glass of champagne.

'What are you doing on St Croix?' a dark-haired woman asked, with expensive bridgework and a slash of red lipstick for a mouth.

'Making a commercial about marriage,' she replied with bitter humour. 'How about you?'

Hunger staved off and champagne liberally supplied, Lauren spent the night in a frenzy of dancing and rather childish party games. When they were all a little jaded at two in the morning, she was implored to take a turn at the microphone and performed a laudable 'The Lady is a Tramp' because she thought it would look startlingly bad in the Press should it come to their ears.

That Ryan thought so too might be the reason he was watching her with eyes as cold as gun metal from a table fifteen feet away. Crooking an imperative finger that didn't expect to be disobeyed, he watched as she passed on the microphone and approached him warily.

'I've been having some fun. Do you mind?' She was deliberately belligerent.

'If this is what amuses you——' he waved a negligent hand at the proceedings, his gaze intimidating '—I shall have to re-educate you. How much champagne have you had?'

'Lots.' She continued to be truculent. 'Don't worry, I won't pass out on you.'

'You won't get the chance.' He was arctic. Standing up, he grasped her elbow in a vice-like grip. 'I find nothing more of a turn-off than a drunken woman making an exhibition of herself. Fortunately you were in good company. I dare say none of them will remember much in the morning.'

'I don't care if they do,' she muttered aggressively, and found herself bundled into a car.

She was shepherded back to their suite with the minimum of civility. He flung her nightdress at her and told her to put it on, indicating the en-suite bathroom with a mocking gesture of his hand. As he pulled at his tie, his attitude told her that he had had enough of her tantrums and wouldn't put up with much more.

Lauren changed, wrenching the scrap of silk over her head, and emerged, eyes glittering, daring him to appreciate the effect.

'What do you want, applause?' His gaze felt like the scratch of a rapier in silent menace over her skin. 'Haven't your talents been appreciated enough for one night?'

'What talents do I possess, Ryan?' Her bravery was slipping away like sand in the wind but she couldn't give in. 'The great Ryan Daniels marrying a chit of a model— and light-fingered to boot. It would keep the City amused for weeks.'

The look in his eyes frightened her and she backed towards the bed as he advanced, unable to keep her balance as he pushed her backwards and she fell against the silken surface, her hair a dark cloud around her head.

'You have a cat's tongue but the claws of a kitten.' Kneeling on the bed, he seized her chin, his gold hair falling over his forehead, the civilised veneer replaced by something more earthily male. 'Shut up and sleep it off or I'll show you how much I dislike being kept waiting.' His mouth cut off any protest she might have made, storming at her brittle pretence of indifference, reminding her heartlessly how fickle were her body's desires.

A breathless sob marked the end of the kiss, Lauren burying her face into the pillow, feeling those hateful fingers smooth her hair back from her face and touch her flushed cheek.

'You have a lot to learn about men.' His voice had a rough edge of regret to it but he said no more. She felt his weight lift from the bed and heard the door close behind him. Despite her conviction that she wouldn't get a moment's rest, she was asleep before he returned to the room.

Lauren awoke the next morning to the presentiment that something very bad had happened. The sun gashed the bed with huge tears of light and her head was thumping in tune to some thoughtless steel band which appeared to be outside the window. Her throat was sore, her feet were sore and she suddenly remembered her descent down the palm tree and realised 'suitable' was not likely to be an appellation she was attributed for some time.

'Good afternoon.' Ryan supplied her with a cup and saucer that seemed brilliantly white and, more thoughtfully, two paracetamols. 'Feeling better?'

'No.' She pulled the sheet up when she realised she was naked and watched him suspiciously from between lowered lashes.

'You can relax,' he said. 'I find your hangover no more alluring than the state you were in last night. I have to go out. If you decide to follow my example, I suggest you use the main entrance; there's a car at your disposal and——' he flung a handful of notes at the bed '—I suggest you take some money.'

Watching him go in mutinous silence, Lauren felt uncomfortable. His scathing attitude to her rebellion made her feel like a naughty schoolgirl. What had he expected? Obedient compliance? Her mind winged to his parents. They dovetailed perfectly. Sir Charles and Lady Daniels were an exemplary match. Had their relationship been founded on love or cold-blooded expediency?

Taking the two tablets, Lauren looked ahead with trepidation. She wondered what Ryan had planned for her. He had said she needed re-educating and she didn't like the sound of that much. She had the feeling that Ryan didn't possess a forgiving nature and remembering the expression in his eyes the night before made her shiver inwardly.

When she began to feel more human, she showered and dressed in cool white cotton. A maid appeared, smiling shyly, and proceeded to restore the crumpled bed to its previous splendour. Lauren retreated to the balcony and spotted the palm tree, her misgivings manifold. It had been rather childish, she reflected, grateful for the arrival of a tray delivering chilled fruit juice clinking with ice-cubes.

Ryan returned, his hair darkened slightly by the heat but still holding the groomed elegance of weathered gold. The hard bones of his face were clothed in bronzed skin that looked sculpted and allowed for no surplus flesh.

His face held a cruel beauty, Lauren speculated, as those light eyes found hers, his thoughts unreadable.

'Have you eaten?' The question was prosaic and she was startled, expecting the battle to begin.

'Oh—er—no.' She saluted him with her glass of fruit juice. 'About last night. I—I realise I behaved badly.' It wasn't easy to apologise, especially considering the fact he had blackmailed her into marriage, but she had her own code of standards to appease. 'You can't expect me to become your wife without some period of adjustment.'

'Wedding nerves?' His smile was thin as he sifted through a handful of post. 'Surprising, considering we've made love before.'

He wasn't going to be denied his pound of flesh, Lauren realised with a sinking heart.

'That was unpremeditated,' she protested, and moved closer to him in unconscious appeal.

'Not by me, it wasn't.' Ryan flicked her a mocking glance. 'I've been thinking of nothing else since I met you.'

'You know what I mean.' She touched his arm. 'Ryan, this isn't going to work; there must be some other way——'

'To keep you out of gaol? I'm afraid not.' His sarcasm was cutting. 'I'm hungry. Get whatever you need; we're going out.'

Bewildered, Lauren collected her purse. Ryan took her hand in his and guided her away from the harbour to maze of small shops, cafés and hotels. It was very different from the tourist haunts she had visited the evening before. It was Saturday and there was an outdoor market where the Cruzan patois rang out in active bartering.

'The influence is largely Danish,' Ryan informed her. 'It came under the auspices of the United States in 1938. He guided her to a café where the seats were in the shade and she sat down gratefully. Her feet were still painful from her dancing bout the night before and her head was still suffering from the ravage of champagne.

'You've got something horrible planned, haven't you?' she accused him.

'Have I?' He ordered the local delicacy—some kind of fish stew. The appetising aroma tempted her after her first dubious perusal and, giving up an attempt to make him reveal her fate, she gingerly tasted the concoction.

'Good gracious!' She sounded and looked astounded. 'It's wonderful.'

'Take my advice; you'll find most things turn out that way.' Ryan actually smiled and Lauren was dazzled, then she realised she was staring and looked away hastily, poking the stew with her spoon.

'What is it?' she asked.

'Kallaloo.' He surveyed her features with analytic precision. 'It's eaten with fungi, and cornmeal boiled with okra. I thought, considering your delicate condition, we'd keep it light.'

'Haven't you ever done anything foolish?' She sat back, unaware of the pleading expression in her eyes. Loath as she was to ingratiate herself, she didn't much like being the subject of his disapproval.

'Yes,' he agreed, not giving an inch. 'The value of experience is learning from it, wouldn't you say?'

'Is that another cryptic clue?' She flicked a strand of hair behind her ear, pretending not to care.

Silvery-blue eyes narrowed slightly. 'If you need time to adjust, we'll play the rest of the honeymoon at your pace. I must add, I don't intend to sleep in the bath or request another room. If you should wish to go back to where we left off before your histrionic flight from the balcony then you will find your wedding dress and other accessories clean and waiting in the wardrobe.'

'That's perverted!' She faltered under his crushing gaze, her cheeks rosy pink. 'You're trying to humiliate me.'

'Humiliation doesn't come at the top of my list of motives. But considering I have to endure gossip about my wife swinging through the palm trees, not to mention your debut as a vocalist with "The Lady is a Tramp", I think you could do with a taste of your own medicine.'

'You don't care what people think.' Her eyes widened at his sudden flaring anger.

'You're wrong there, darling. I prefer my private life to stay that way. And, just as a matter of fine detail, the bodice I want open and your hair down——'

'Never!' She pushed away her dish, looking away, unable to bear the determination in his eyes.

'I said I'd be patient.'

'You'll have to be.'

His lips pursed thoughtfully. 'It's amazing what a hot Caribbean night can do to the determination. Even in a kingsize bed it's hard to stop touching.'

'You——!' She stood up but his soft murmur of her name made her wait with forced patience. He paid the bill and rose leisurely, catching her hand and securing it with his own.

'You didn't eat much,' he commented, totally in command of the situation.

'That's hardly surprising.' She cast him a malignant glance. 'I suppose you're fireproof when it comes to Caribbean nights and restricted bed space.'

'Not at all, but I have every faith in your capitulation.' He smiled as if he was remembering something that pleased him.

Lauren lay wide awake, watching the harbour lights through the thin gauze around the bed. It was warm and

Ryan had left the slatted doors open to let the cool air circulate. They had spent the day touring the island, and she was dog-tired, but sleep evaded her.

She let her mind wander over her conversation with the man lying next to her. He had called her an emotional vandal and she couldn't help thinking he was right. True, the robbery had put her in an untenable position, but she had reacted to Ryan as a sexual threat—challenge— since the first moment they had met. Unfortunately for her she had neither the experience nor the natural guile to play the sophisticated love game her husband was used to. For him she was a diversion. He was bored with the Chantal Rabannes of the world and no doubt in time he would get bored with her too. The thought made her angry. She disliked being some transitory pleasure in the life of a powerful man.

Lauren froze as the bed dipped, but she refused to look round when she heard him moving about the room. She heard the clink of glass and realised she was thirsty.

'Planning to run away to sea?' His voice had a provoking note to it and she yelped as the cold glass was placed against her back. 'Drink?' he enquired smoothly.

'What is it?' She sat up, holding the white sheet against her shoulder as she took the glass.

'Orange juice. Nothing alcoholic, in case you were worried.'

'Ha, ha.' She drank thirstily, wishing he weren't there and she could strip off and sleep without the covers. Despite the air coming in from the balcony, it was still too warm for anything but the lightest cover. Putting the glass down on the bedside cabinet, she turned away from him, thumping her pillow, revealing the frustration she felt with the situation.

She nearly shot out of bed when his hand curled around her neck and his thumb probed the stiff muscles at its base.

'Want me to help you sleep?' he offered, his voice devoid of expression.

'What had you in mind?' she queried sceptically.

'Lie on your stomach,' he instructed, smiling at the telling turn of her head. 'I promise I have no ulterior motives.'

She lay down as he asked, guessing his intention and determined to bear it if he could. She sighed as he began to massage the tight muscles of her neck and shoulders. There was something delectable about indulging in Ryan's touch knowing full well she had no intention of complying with his terms and that without her capitulation he would take matters no further. The scrap of silk with bootlace straps she wore allowed him access to most of her back.

'You're good at this.' Lauren's eyes narrowed in drowsy appreciation. 'I suppose you've had plenty of practice.'

'I don't usually try and send my lover to sleep,' he remarked drily. 'But you're irritating me fidgeting all the time.'

Lauren shrugged him off, turning to face him, tired, cross and hurt by his attitude. 'Why didn't you marry one of your fabulous lovers, then? Chantal Rabanne is dying of mortification because you lowered yourself to marry me.'

His teeth gleamed in silent laughter. 'Chantal would certainly have been a tamer proposition.'

'You deserve her!' She felt wild with hurt anger, wanting to lash out at his cool amusement.

'No.' He was suddenly serious. 'I think I very probably deserve you.'

'Well, I know that isn't a compliment.' She got out of bed and went to the open balcony doors, the breeze blowing her hair back from her face so that it fanned over her shoulders.

Getting up, he came to stand behind her, his hands gripping her waist tightly and making her jump with surprise.

'Who did you call today? Derek!' he grated.

She was stunned that he should know she had tried to contact her brother. 'Are you having me watched?' Turning on him furiously, she found her thighs meeting the cold metal of the balcony rail as he refused to give way.

'Why not?' he enquired, infuriating her. 'I don't trust you an inch.'

He had made his feelings plain but his mistrust still hurt. Tears stung her eyes. She had revealed her secrets to him, allowed him the intimacy of her body, and he still suspected her of the utmost duplicity.

'You're lucky I'm innocent,' she scorned him. 'You've made yourself very vulnerable giving a suspected thief your name. That wouldn't impress the board, would it, Ryan?'

'Don't threaten me, Lauren.' He spoke quietly but his voice made her shiver. 'If it makes you feel any better, there are very few people I do trust.'

Her eyes darkened with scorn. 'What a delightful world you inhabit.'

'We inhabit,' he reminded her.

'We?' She stared at the shadowed features of his face. Pushing a perplexed hand through the thick sheaf of hair falling across her eyes, she was unaware that the movement drew the silk tight over her breasts.

Ryan's only apparel, a pair of powder-blue shorts, left most of his body bare. She was far too tense to go back to bed and lie passively beside him.

'Come to bed. I'll calm you down. It worked last time,' he responded as her head jerked to attention.

'I'd rather sleep on bare boards.'

'Try the couch,' he invited. 'If you leave the suite I'll drag you back by your hair.'

He viewed her surprise at his capitulation with demonic amusement as she approached the bed and grabbed a pillow, her frame rigid with prim reproof as she stalked from the bedroom. His laughter was her undoing. Without thought she turned on her heel and swung the pillow in an arc, aiming at his head. She landed two good blows before Ryan caught her, lifting her easily and subduing her wild threshing with an economy of movements that was humiliating. The breath rushed out of her lungs as he crushed her beneath him.

'Given up on your bridal fantasy?' she gibed, catching a handful of his hair and pulling hard.

'Oh, that.' His forearm across her throat restricted her ability to move and her fingers lost their grip, her body shamefully aware of the muscular strength holding her down and, even more scandalously, enjoying it. 'It seemed a practical way to keep you in my bedroom— where I want you.'

She stilled, realising she had fallen into his trap without a single vestige of suspicion. His unacceptable terms had made her feel safe with him, made her stay rather than run as she had the night before.

'I would have thought rape too barbaric for your civilised taste,' she panted hotly, trying to calm the heat in her loins as his body moved against hers intimately.

'Grow up.' His tone was scathing, his breath beating against her cheek. 'You can't share this bed without making love any more than I can.'

'I'm prepared to sleep elsewhere.' Her face caught fire as her hips lifted against his in a small involuntary movement, her lips parting as she tried to stifle her response.

'Sleep is overrated.' Ryan's mouth drifted lazily over hers. 'Why didn't you keep going if you wanted to leave?'

Lauren gazed up at him non-comprehendingly. He made her protests sound like ritual skirmishes in some kind of mating game. Clutching at his shoulders, she felt the strength in him bearing down on her, wishing her mind wouldn't fill with cotton wool and find his maleness fascinating.

Sensing her weakening, Ryan took her mouth, kissing her deeply, chasing the reluctant spark of response and fanning it with ruthless intent. Lauren made an attempt to rebuff him, her head moving restlessly against the pillow, her body arching as he pushed up the scrap of flowered silk and his hand moved caressingly over her breast.

What did it matter? a traitorous voice silked through Lauren's dazed mind. Why deny herself this magical pleasure? Ryan felt the change in her touch as her fingers relaxed their grip and spread out caressingly against his skin. Kissing her softly, he raised his head to view the passionate rebellion marking her features. Her mouth, slightly swollen and pouting, drew him back to lick the delicious curves before he bit a kiss into the join of her neck, hearing her husky cry with a quickening of his senses. Stripping her with what little patience he had left, Ryan pressed burning kisses over her body, his hands shaping the delicate ribcage, cupping her breasts and arousing the tiny rosy crests with the tip of his tongue.

'Ryan—no.' The feeling he was creating threatened to engulf her and she pushed against him, surprised to find herself pulled on top of him, his fingers running through her dark mane of hair.

'No, what?' He ran his hands over her thighs, appreciating the tightness of her buttocks. 'Going somewhere?'

Her breasts heaved with the force of her emotions. She wanted to strangle him and love him at the same time. Her fingers slid over the roughness of his jaw as she took the initiative and her mouth dictated to the firmness of his, her body in languorous motion as he caressed the length of her back, making shivers scurry up and down her spine.

Hooking her fingers under the waistband of his shorts, Lauren tugged at the thin cotton to find Ryan watching her with an expression in his eyes that scalded her. As he kissed her, the moment was lost in a sensation of feeling, Lauren shivering with fierce reaction as he pushed her back and eased her thighs apart, leaving her in little doubt as to his arousal and desire for swift release. She had invited and wanted the surging strength of his desire, trembling at the hard push of his body against hers. She cried out as he took her, needles of golden fire, shooting like stars, dissolving her mortal frame until she was ablaze, lightning ripping her apart, the golden meld of muscle and bone holding her to the earth, fused with hers in a crescendo of pleasure.

Lauren spent the rest of the night a slave, giving mindlessly whatever he asked. When he let her sleep, she slept dreamlessly, her body perfectly at peace with itself, cocooned in a delicious exhaustion.

Ryan watched her, his fingers brushing back the dark hair and looping it behind her ear.

'Sweet sleep of innocence,' he murmured to himself, his mouth twisting with self-derision as he eased away and lay back, looking at the ceiling. Putting his forearm over his eyes, he resisted the temptation to dwell on her beauty. She existed for him in a primitive corner of his mind; if he allowed her to taint his every waking thought—the consequences were unimaginable.

CHAPTER SEVEN

LAUREN endured the remaining week of the cruise, having been welcomed back to the *Halcyon* with speculative interest by many of the guests and thinly veiled hostility by most of the Rabanne family. Her relationship with Ryan settled into an uneasy truce. He was as conscious as she that the *Halcyon* was too public a venue for one of their spats and decided to play a waiting game. Equally, Lauren resolved to wait until their return to London before she challenged him to reveal what he knew of the espionage business. If he wasn't going to prosecute either Derek or herself then he must have someone else in mind, and if that was true, he had blackmailed her into marriage under false pretences. But even this knowledge wasn't sufficient to harden her resistance. The nights didn't get any cooler and the bed on the cruiser was considerably smaller than the one they had shared in their honeymoon hotel. Despite her resolve that Ryan wouldn't have a willing bedmate, she suffered a mortifying set-back when, in the depths of sleep, she turned to him and what had started as a pleasant dream turned into passionate reality.

The return to the Daniels mansion marginally increased their privacy but Lauren was all too aware of the ever-present staff. Bannister loomed whenever he was wanted as if some sixth sense alerted him. She had hoped Ryan's suite would have matching divans but the large four-poster defeated her hopes.

'Don't worry, it's well sprung.' Ryan chose to interpret her downcast expression as a reflection on the antiquity of the bed rather than the fact that she would have to share it with him.

'I'd rather have a bed of my own,' she retorted frigidly, the familiar warmth in his eyes confounding her.

'Then you'd have to sleepwalk to get at me.' Ryan pretended to consider the idea. 'Not just turn, run your hands over me and breathe, "Ryan."'

'If you weren't in such proximity, it wouldn't happen.' Lauren hated her own weakness but didn't bother going through the motions of denying the incident.

'In that case you can hardly expect me to be enthusiastic about separate beds.' Walking towards her, he deliberately began to pull at the studs on his pale grey denim shirt, watching the colour come into her cheeks and her eyes stay determinedly on his face. 'Besides, I like to know where you are. It saves me the trouble of coming to find you.'

Lauren bit her lip to fight back the torrent of words that threatened to plead her innocence for the umpteenth time.

'This marriage is a farce,' she raged emotionally. 'What am I supposed to do? Stay incarcerated in this house playing Mrs Daniels? Your mother has the place running like clockwork—there's absolutely nothing to do!'

Ryan considered this, continuing to undress, pulling his shirt out of the waistband of the light cotton trousers he had chosen to travel in.

'I thought you wanted to design clothes.' Shedding the shirt, he fingered the neckline of the pink pastel sweater she was wearing with a short candy-striped cotton skirt. 'I don't want you to continue modelling but I am prepared to back your designs. Find yourself somewhere to work and you're in business.'

'But that will cost a fortune!' she protested, her hand coming up to catch his as his fingers dipped into the well of her collarbone.

'It's my money to give.' His gaze was intensified by the deep set of his eyes, blue sparks glimmering like hints of summer in a grey sky. 'You can thank me if you want to.' His mouth grazed hers and she pulled back angrily, wishing she weren't tempted.

'We'll be late for dinner,' she pointed out, trying to keep her voice level. 'You were in the process of getting changed, weren't you?' Her eyes told him she knew exactly what he was doing, tempting her with his body, and that she was having none of it.

'Nothing quite so prosaic.' He viewed her indolently. 'What scam are you working now, Lauren? You've got me confused.'

'Scam?' She was incensed. 'If I were the immoral creature you imagine, I'd jump into bed with you and take you for every penny I could. I know you can't get this through your thick head——' she put her hands on her hips, glaring at him '—but I'd give my right arm to put the clock back three weeks and turn down the modelling assignment at your damn factory!'

Ryan's eyebrows lifted sceptically. 'I can believe it. Getting caught has that effect.'

Her hand whipped to his face and she slapped him before he had the chance to subdue her. He hauled her into the hard strength of his body, and her eyes widened at the violence in his.

'If I hadn't promised myself I'd save you from any repetition of the past, I'd make you regret that.' He pushed her away from him abruptly and slammed into the bathroom, leaving Lauren to tremble in the aftermath of the encounter.

It hadn't occurred to her that Ryan's willingness to let her dictate their love life had anything to do with what she had told him about her past. The thought unsettled her; it showed aspects of caring and consideration that she didn't credit him with possessing. She wanted to ask him a thousand questions but when he escorted her to dinner he was coldly polite and she found him as approachable as an iceberg.

It was how to tackle Ryan that creased her brow into a frown as she peered around the gloom of the Docklands warehouse she was viewing as a prospective workshop. The agent found the mechanism for opening the skylight blinds and the place flooded with bright spring sunshine, dust motes dancing wildly as if freed from the darkness.

'It needs cleaning,' she commented dubiously, scanning the bare boards and the blank expanse of wall. 'And decorating.'

'The view is stunning.' The agent managed to pull back the slats that showed the Thames snaking into the distance below.

Lauren smiled. Yes, the view was definitely worth something.

Footsteps made her turn her head to see Ryan entering the property, his hair catching the light and glinting with streaks of gold. He had arranged to view the warehouse with her and she assumed some matter of business had made him late.

Glancing at his watch as if wondering how quickly he could be away, he gave the place a cursory glance. 'What do you think?' He was brief.

'It has possibilities.' She gave him a dismissive look, finding his attitude abrasive. He epitomised power-dressing, his navy suit and impeccable linen reminding Lauren of the first time they had met.

'Ah, Mr Daniels.' The agent appeared to rejuvenate before her eyes. 'I'm sure you'll agree it's a property that could be made very desirable given a little effort.'

'Given a little interior decorator,' he mocked, sending an assessing glance at Lauren. 'It's not me you have to convince—my wife knows what she needs for her business, I just sign the cheque.'

Giving him a killing look, Lauren went again to the panoramic view of the Thames. Ryan's offer to back her fashion aspirations made her feel uneasy; it felt like a pay-off for a lifetime of playing wife to Ryan Daniels.

The agent's mouth depressed; her back view didn't look very promising.

'Maybe you could give us a little time to reflect,' Ryan interposed smoothly. 'I can have the keys returned to your office in an hour.'

'Yes, of course, Mr Daniels.' The man was glad to leave, not comfortable with other people's domestic battles.

'"Yes, of course, Mr Daniels",' Lauren mimicked when the door closed behind the man. 'If I'd come on my own, I wouldn't have got through the door, never mind been left with the keys.'

'Of course you would, darling. Lauren Daniels will be welcomed wherever my family's name is known. It comes with the job.'

'The job that comes in a higher bracket than "mistress", do you mean?' she queried sweetly, her green eyes firing as she remained where she was.

'I hardly see our marriage as a sexual barter.' He came to stand beside her, giving the Thames a brief glance before turning to face her, leaning back against the glass. 'More like a protection racket.' He smiled as if the thought amused him.

'You blackmailed me into marriage for my own protection?' She gave a brief laugh. 'Very amusing.'

'Your track record wasn't impressive. One suspected theft, caught red-handed in my cabin, the victim of two separate incidents of underworld larceny. I don't want to see your pretty face swollen with bruises——' his fingers brushed her profile and she glared at him angrily '—by thieves who think you've double-crossed them or anyone you happen to think worthy of a bout of amateur detection.'

'And this protection of yours...' She saw her chance to put the record straight. 'Presumably you have an idea whom I'm being protected against?'

'Mmm.' He smiled, amused at her frustration. 'What do you think of this place? It looks the part—or could, if you put your mind to it.'

'I'd decorate it myself.' She was momentarily distracted.

Sizing her up, he looked at the high ceilings and then raised a quizzical eyebrow. 'I'd rather you didn't break your neck decorating and I hate the smell of turps.'

'I meant the design.' She was impatient. 'Anyway, I'm not sure I want to borrow money from you. It's a high-risk business——'

'I'd take the risk; I happen to think you're remarkably talented,' he cut in.

Giving him a look that spoke volumes, she refused to be distracted. 'Tell me who you think framed me.' She tugged at the lapels of his jacket, demanding he return to the point.

'It is only a suspicion. I'm still awaiting evidence to make the final link. That sort of information in your hands would be extremely dangerous.' He removed her fingers, brushing out the creases she had made.

Folding the keys in her hand, he gave the warehouse a final glance. 'Ring me if you decide to take the place. I won't be at dinner tonight—I have another engagement.'

She watched him leave, surprised to realise that the pain in her palm was caused by her grip on the keys. So, he suspected someone of being involved in espionage and yet he gave her no apology for the accusations thrown her way. It struck her that the reason he wouldn't tell her was that he still suspected her of being in cahoots with the villain of the piece. Violent anger raged through her. She wanted to follow him back to his office and demand to know where she stood—but the next minute she realised how futile that was. Ryan wouldn't tell her anything he didn't want her to know. He would give her one look out of those cold, steely eyes, silently telling her she was misbehaving, and retribution would be swift and that would be the end of it.

Lady Daniels was very interested in all the details of Lauren's enterprise. They had adjourned to the elegant room Lauren had used upon her first visit to the house. The pale yellow walls gleamed under the mock Victorian wall-lights, the two women poring over drawings of the prospective warehouse conversion.

'The ceiling is raftered with huge skylights,' she reported. 'I'd like to use the light and keep it spartan. I dislike all that fussy clutter that goes with the well known salons.'

'There's nothing wrong with creating your own style,' her mother-in-law agreed. 'What did Ryan think of it?'

Lauren paused, trying to think of a polite answer. 'I don't think he cared particularly; he sees his role as paymaster.'

'How irritating.' Lady Daniels shared a knowing look with the younger woman and they both laughed.

Lauren had plenty of time to reflect on her husband's shortcomings that night, lying awake waiting for him to come in. She went to sleep just before dawn and had a hazy recollection of someone in the room moving about when she woke. Ryan's navy suit was waiting to be taken for dry-cleaning, Lauren noted, heavy-eyed and bad-tempered. There was no sign of her husband and, upon questioning Tina, her maid, she discovered he had left the house at eight o'clock, presumably for the office.

Leaving a message with his secretary, telling him she had decided on the warehouse, some imp of mischief made her add that she wouldn't be home for dinner as she had another engagement. Why she should deem such tit-for-tat behaviour necessary she didn't bother to question.

Arranging to have lunch with Marisa Lasalle, she spent the morning ringing around for quotes for decorating the dinosaur of a building she had taken on.

She met her friend in Covent Garden and they had lunch in a pub overlooking the square where street entertainers amused the crowds. Discussing her launch into the fashion world, Marisa informed her that Fi Markham, a temperamental friend of theirs, was looking for an opening. Lauren needed an assistant and Fi was a wonder with the scissors. She mentally stored the information away, wishing her new venture would absorb her the way it would have done before she met Ryan Daniels.

Why had he stayed out all night? It could be business, of course, she pondered; either that or one of his old flames had turned on the magic. The thought took root and she found herself possessed by a black rage that made her collect herself hastily. To actually care what Ryan did was the road to perdition. She resolved not to question him on the subject, wishing she hadn't left that childish message with his secretary. She was committed to spending the evening elsewhere now.

That afternoon Lauren determinedly visited various retailers, browsing among bolts of cloth, her imagination transforming them into her own designs. Upon previous visits her eye had always been half on her budget—it was hard to shake loose the restraints of stringent economy.

When she arrived back at her old home, Derek smiled in greeting, moving to pick up the ringing phone. 'Did you know Ryan's looking for you?' he queried, startled as she tugged the plug out of the wall, cutting him off.

'Is he? Why?'

'I don't know; he didn't say.'

'Then it can't be very important, can it?' She smiled winningly. 'Coffee?'

'I'll make some.' Derek's ordered mind found his sister's capricious attitude puzzling. 'It won't take you a second——'

'To ring in and report to his secretary? No, thanks. Anyway, I left a message earlier. Don't worry, I'll take full responsibility.'

Derek grinned suddenly, shaking his head. 'He's got his hands full with you. At work, he speaks, everyone jumps—including me.'

'Well, I'm not an employee, am I?' She tried to eradicate any hint of bitterness from her tone. She was a rich man's whim, Ryan's latest pet, to be teased and tortured until she gave in and whimpered at his ankles.

Sharing a pizza with her brother, she stayed until nine and then accepted a lift back to the Daniels mansion.

Bannister opened the door to admit her, a caution in his eyes that told her he had been instructed to report on her return.

'Ryan's in, I take it?' She winced at the affirmative nod, feeling like a schoolgirl sneaking back after 'lights out'.

Pushing her hair back over her shoulders, she made for the sound of voices. To say she felt out of place would be an understatement. Dressed in a suede skirt and jacket she had worn for her lunch date, she was woefully inadequate compared to the display of elegantly decked figures dripping with jewellery.

'Ah, Lauren.' Lady Daniels was polite as usual. 'I'm sorry, my dear, I forgot to tell you I was having a dinner party tonight. I did tell Ryan but he was unable to contact you.'

'I'll get changed.' She smiled glassily, retreating from the battery of eyes.

Working as a model, Lauren had learnt the art of the quick change. Her dress captured gypsy magic, an abstract print that suggested summer was near, a concept particularly welcome in March. She joined the party just as the men were filtering out of their domain to join the ladies.

Giving Ryan a quick glance, she hastily lowered her lashes, not proof against the direct, assessing quality of those silver-blue eyes.

'Darling.' The endearment was used as a greeting, the brush of his lips against her cheek perfunctory. 'Busy day?'

'Yes.' Her reply was non-committal, for she was conscious of his fingers lightly clasping her waist as he walked with her to the drawing-room.

Lauren was kept busy answering questions about her wedding and honeymoon. Ryan remained at her side for a decent interval and then gravitated to the far end of the room, spending at least an hour in deep conversation with a stunning blonde.

At first Lauren merely kept track of where he was as a defence mechanism. She couldn't believe, with his impeccable manners, he would blatantly flirt with another woman days after returning from his honeymoon. Seeing was believing!

Lauren had always considered herself even-tempered, but Ryan Daniels had introduced her to parts of her personality she hadn't known she possessed. Jealousy boiled in her blood, her eyes venomous when they met Ryan's across the room. The last thing she wanted was for him to know how she felt, but her emotions were too new to disguise. As if summoned, Ryan made his way back to her and stayed at her side for the rest of the evening. It did little to soothe her ravaging emotions.

Sir Charles and Lady Daniels invited them to have a nightcap and Lauren had to endure sharing the couch with him as he took time with his brandy, relaxed and easy in his parents' company.

'Was that Diana Palmer you were talking to?' Lady Daniels asked her son, with an almost imperceptible tightening of her lips as Lauren glared in Ryan's direction.

'Yes, she's just got back from the States. Have you met Diana in your line of work?' Ryan turned to view his wife's set features with a commendable lack of expression. 'I would have introduced you but I had the feeling you disliked her for some reason.'

'Why should I dislike her?' Lauren responded with as much pride as she could muster. 'We've never met.' Rising to her feet, she excused herself to Ryan's parents, leaving the room with a backward glance at Ryan that left nothing unsaid. Closing the door with a much tried for lack of violence, she then heard Elizabeth reprimand her son.

'You shouldn't have brought Diana Palmer here. What possessed you to invite her...?'

What possessed Ryan to do anything? Lauren seethed as she marched up the stairs. Why had he married her to humiliate her a fortnight later with some beauty from his past? It didn't make sense. She had assumed Ryan had asked her to be his wife because he was driven by ungovernable lust. He had indicated that, telling her she was his perfect woman, that she intrigued him. Had he tired of her so quickly or had he been playing another game all along?

Lauren's thoughts were in turmoil. She waited for him, pacing up and down the length of their bedroom suite, her green eyes glittering frenetically. She couldn't believe he wouldn't come, that he could leave her tormented and miserable. She heard footsteps as Sir Charles and Lady Daniels made for their rooms and waited until they had passed. In an agony of indecision, she then ran to her wardrobe, flinging it open, gathering up an armful of clothes before she realised that she hadn't a suitcase handy to pack them into. With a sob of frustration, she flung them on to the bed, pushing a hand through her hair, revealing the vulnerable expression in her eyes.

Impulsively, she left the room and ran lightly down the stairs, pausing as she saw Bannister.

'Bannister, will you get me a suitcase?'

'I'm very sorry, madam, but Mr Ryan gave instructions to the contrary. I believe he's in his study if you wish to discuss the matter with him.'

'I believe I will,' she muttered under her breath, and saw a glimmer of humour for a moment lighten the butler's dignified countenance.

Ryan looked up from his work as she entered, his eyes quick to assess her mood, and he capped his pen with the deliberation of someone who had a reservoir of patience that was quickly becoming used up.

'You look full of hell,' he commented provocatively. 'Is the bed too big for you and Peggit?'

'This house is too small for you and me,' she returned hostilely. 'I understand I'm not allowed to leave.'

He glanced at his watch with infuriating practicality. 'It's two in the morning. Where would you go? I shouldn't advise crossing London alone at this time of night; it isn't safe.'

'And you do care for my safety, don't you, Ryan?' Lauren was vitriolic. 'I wonder why?'

'Don't be tiresome,' he murmured dismissively. 'Go back to bed; I won't disturb you.'

Lauren had never met a man who made her feel so physically violent. Her eyes burnt with an inner heat barely quenched by the cool grey stare that returned her gaze calmly.

'Why?' She walked around the desk and surprised him by perching on the edge facing him. 'You've always been keen to disturb me before.'

Ryan leant back in his seat with barely suppressed irritation. 'I understood you wanted to sleep alone. Are you telling me you've changed your mind?'

'No—I——' She regarded him with deep resentment. How did he manage to make her go on the defensive? She was the one with a grievance. 'We may not have a conventional marriage but I won't be humiliated in public. I might be rusty in social etiquette——' she got into her stride with a vengeance '—but even I know a newly married man does not spend the whole evening chatting up a man-eating blonde.'

Ryan's slow smile played havoc with her senses. 'That bothered you, did it?'

It so obviously had that Lauren couldn't find the words to effectively deny it.

'I don't care what you do in private,' she recovered valiantly, wishing she spoke the truth. 'I'd be grateful if you found solace elsewhere.'

'Liar,' he taunted her. 'You were searching the bed for me this morning—I watched you. By the state of the bed I'd guess you had a restless night.'

'You're making it up!' she accused, pushing herself off the edge of his desk, too agitated to sit still. 'I won't listen!'

Catching her wrist, Ryan caused her to overbalance, but he caught her, lifting her on to his knee.

'It's about time you listened,' Ryan growled feelingly as she squirmed against him.

'Let go of me,' she spat up into his face, hot with shock as his hand skimmed her calf and caressed her thigh in one smooth, piratical movement.

'Why? We both know what you want. You want me to kiss you senseless so that you can fool yourself into believing that you were unwilling.' Lauren quivered at the intensity of desire she witnessed in his gaze. 'I'm very tempted to make it easy for you.'

'And spoil your splendid record of making things difficult?' she retorted. She was breathing shallowly, aware of his hand warm against her outer thigh, his fingertips drawing small, lazy circles against her skin. Aware of imminent danger, Lauren realised she was a hair's breadth from confirming everything he had said. Her body had relaxed against his, she had barely protested against the liberties he was taking with her thigh and she was in the grip of trembling anticipation at the thought of what he would do next. Suddenly it was imperative that she knew just what was going on between Ryan and the exotic blonde model.

'Was—is Diana Palmer——?' She failed to finish the sentence, as Ryan covered her mouth with his in a fusion of explosive intimacy.

The driving force of his passion should have repelled her but instead it gave her reassurance. Her lips were shaped and moulded by his, the red-hot silk of his tongue tracing the white cutting edge of her teeth with audacious confidence, leaving her weak to attack. Her lashes flickered as he trapped her between his body and the wing of the chair, but his mouth provided a burning focus, scorching hers, biting at the soft, trembling curves until she gave way and allowed him access to the honeyed recesses, shuddering as he coaxed her into returning the seductive caress of his tongue.

Jealousy had torn at her defences, leaving them frail and ragged. The threat of another woman made her needs magnify until her pride seemed a poor, worthless thing not worth pursuing.

Her fingers clenched in his shirt, tugging at the fastenings until she could slide her hands into the warmth between linen and skin. Caressing the moulded build of his chest, she let her fingers glide over his ribs, feeling the pant of his diagphragm and the urgent thud of his heart. It was a constant source of wonder to her that Ryan, so impeccably perfect in evening clothes, could shed his civilised, ultra-smooth self and become so sexually compelling. Breaking free from his mouth, her lips traced his breastbone, and she shivered as he gathered up her hair, his fingers caressing her nape, disturbing the downy hair, and travelling on to stroke the line of her spine revealed by the dress.

'Shall we continue this upstairs?' Ryan's voice was roughened by passion.

Lauren felt a moment's satisfaction, knowing that only she absorbed him now; his gaze was latent with sexual intention, and sparks of blue flame were licking at the dry tinder of her passion, igniting an explosion of feeling within her.

Tilting up her face, he feathered her chin with this thumb, bending to place a kiss below her collarbone.

'Was she your girlfriend?' she whispered into the dark gold of his hair as he moved on to the join of her neck, his teeth nipping her in retribution.

'A gentleman never talks about his lovers, Lauren.' He lifted his head, watching his thumb ease the sting where his teeth had marked her flesh. 'Especially to his wife.'

'I'm not your wife,' she protested. 'Not in that way. You've never pretended you loved me. Why do you have to lie about her?'

'You are my wife,' he corrected her, his eyes meeting hers demandingly. 'If you're worried about me breaking my vows, perhaps you should set an example. You seem a little reluctant to keep yours.'

'Don't you think about anything else but sex?' She struggled free, denying the throb of her senses.

'I was thinking about work until you marched in here.' He surveyed her heaving breasts and the passionate glow in her eyes with glittering frustration. 'Was there anything else?'

'Nothing included in your programming.' With a hurt glare, she left the room, slamming the door, ignoring Bannister's shudder as she swept past him and went back upstairs, promising herself that she wouldn't spend another night under the same roof as Ryan.

The next morning, she packed her things into some black plastic bin-liners Tina found for her. The young maid was only temporarily in service, awaiting a place at university, and was less hidebound than the rest of the staff. Ordering a taxi, Lauren managed to escape before any of the other servants alerted the Daniels. Knowing that going back to her own flat would only embroil her brother in her troubles, she decided to go to the warehouse. It had a bedroom and all the usual conveniences—it was the main studio that needed the work.

She spent the morning getting in provisions, from the narrow camp bed to various cleaning materials. She was surprised to find Tina on the doorstep when she returned.

'Mr Ryan,' she commented, tongue-in-cheek, 'said I was more appropriately placed on your payroll than his. Can you afford me?'

'Did he fire you?' Lauren was appalled, green eyes flashing. 'I suppose I can afford you; he's paying the bills, anyway.' Small recompense, she thought vehemently, for what he'd done to her. 'This isn't the Danielses' place, though; it needs a lot of work.'

'It will equip me for college.' Tina followed Lauren to the kitchen, which was uniformly grey, the kitchen units shiny metallic. 'Someone was trying to make a statement.' She giggled at Lauren's appalled look.

'Did Ryan say anything else?' she asked, burying into the bag that contained an electric kettle and pretending not to care.

'He said he'd catch up with you later.' Tina swallowed a giggle. 'When you've—er—got over your tantrum.'

Lauren banged the kettle down on the grey surface, pretending it was Ryan's head. Tantrum! The way she felt was hardly described by that small word. She had confronted him, wanting reassurance. Reassurance! About what? It came on her with a rush of cold fear that what she had really wanted was for Ryan to tell her Diana Palmer didn't matter. That she, Lauren, was the only woman in his life. And why she wanted that was as simple as ABC. She loved him. Loved that smug, self-satisfied, supercilious automaton whose ability to drive her crazy exceeded her worse nightmares.

Viewing Lauren's loss of colour, Tina set about making some coffee. They spent the rest of the day cleaning out the cupboards and washing the paintwork of the living quarters. Tina left at five after the hardest day she had ever spent in service and Lauren was left alone in the huge empty building with the camp bed her only piece of furniture.

She must have slept, because she jerked into consciousness hearing a noise that clearly indicated she was not alone. Sitting up quickly, she overbalanced the camp bed and hit the floor with a thud, her limbs tangled in the sleeping-bag which she was using for a cover.

'From riches to rags in a day.' Ryan's voice mocked her from the doorway. 'Most people fight to go up the social scale, but you're a true rebel, angel.'

'What do you want?' She viewed him hostilely, resenting the fact that he didn't move to help her although she would have repulsed him if he had tried.

'I thought you might like to go out to celebrate but——' he viewed her dishevelled appearance '—it occurred to me you might be a little tired. So I thought we'd eat here.'

'Here?' she echoed, too surprised to consider whether she wished to endure his presence for any length of time.

'It's hardly Claridge's,' he agreed, 'but you appear to like the place.'

'What are we celebrating?' Bewildered, she followed him through to the studio area, her mouth hardening as she viewed the picnic table and chairs, the candle and selection of foil packets. There was even a bottle of champagne.

'You see before you the new president of the Daniels Corporation.' He met her eyes with an air of mock puzzlement in his. 'Aren't you going to congratulate me, darling? You did help in your own small way.'

Running her hands through her hair in a perplexed gesture, Lauren viewed his tall, lean figure with bitter animosity.

'Congratulations.' Her tone was dismissive. 'I suppose I've served my purpose; you've got what you want.'

'You do paint me very black.' He undid the wire fastening on the champagne, the fading view of the Thames a backdrop to the romantic sham he had concocted. He was wearing a black jacket and trousers with a navy blue denim shirt suitable for a wine bar for the yuppy set. Her own crumpled multi-coloured trousers and pink sweatshirt made her feel at a distinct disadvantage.

He handed her a glass of champagne and pulled her seat back, waiting for her to sit down. Lauren hadn't eaten all day and the faint aroma of food made her stomach protest her neglect. She allowed him to seat her, her body stiff with reluctance.

'There will, of course, be a formal acknowledgement of my new position. I'll need you to attend for that. I have promised to finance your fashion aspirations—that will continue. Anything else we have to cover?' he asked.

Lauren couldn't believe he could be so cold! 'Just the little matter of my being falsely accused, Ryan. Have you forgotten about that?' she replied.

'That as yet remains unresolved, but I expect the matter to be cleared up within a very short time now.' Taking a mouthful of champagne, Ryan studied her over the rim. 'If you can't bring yourself to remain with me until then, it might be better if you went back to your brother's place.'

Lauren felt her spine prickle with apprehension. 'You're just trying to frighten me.'

'No,' he said quietly. 'I'm not.'

'But nobody can believe I'm involved—the villains anyway. I know you can't bring yourself to trust me.' She gave him an angry look.

'It's your relationship to me that puts you in danger,' Ryan informed her bluntly. 'I'm well protected, you are not. In this particular board game, you are my queen and you've made yourself vulnerable coming here.'

'I'm surprised you care what happens to me.' She hated the cry for attention in her voice, wishing she could be as clinical about the whole thing as he was.

'Your emotions are still very raw, Lauren. We both need things from our relationship we're not getting. Now isn't the time to resolve that. I can't have you disappearing all the time. I intend to win this particular fight without any casualties.'

'You provoke me.' She sipped her champagne, avoiding his eyes.

'I'll try not to,' he promised solemnly, with a dry humour she failed to understand. 'Let's put the whole thing on ice until this is over.'

She nodded and he touched her champagne glass with his in silent salute. He had his way; they had their candle-lit dinner and he had the truce he wanted. What lay in the future was anyone's guess; Lauren was enough of an ostrich not to want to look too far ahead and enough of a fool to agree to return to the Daniels household.

CHAPTER EIGHT

LAUREN marshalled her staff as they began to make the preparations for the advertising campaign promoting a range of power tools. Ryan had given her the opportunity to design the outfits for one of the Daniels Corporation's publicity campaigns. It was high-tech meeting youth and vigour, giving essentially DIY equipment a sexy image.

They had been allocated one of the executive offices at Daniels and Blackthorn and it wasn't until Richard Harrington dropped in that Lauren realised whose it was.

'It doesn't pay to lose against Daniels,' he murmured drolly, watching the make-up team work on the models. 'I suppose its better than being given the office next to the boiler.'

'I didn't realise.' Lauren was mortified. 'Really, I had no idea.'

'No?' He smiled with a little shrug. 'Time I moved on anyway. It's the name of the game in this kind of business. You don't stay to fight your corner; the opposition tends to be ruthless.'

Lauren couldn't deny that quality in Ryan. She believed him adept at manipulating people. She was surprised Harrington had decided to remain as long as he had, but she expected there was a certain protocol governing this sort of thing, probably involving a golden handshake.

'I'll let you get on.' He gave her an embarrassed little smile as if he wished he hadn't said as much as he had, and left. Another victim of Ryan's charm—she watched him go feeling a certain affinity with the man. She, too, had got embroiled in Ryan's machinations and she felt a similar feeling of bewilderment. Richard Harrington had lost his fiancée and his prospects in a very short period of time, and Lauren wasn't unaware of the fact that Ryan's acceptance of Derek as his sister's new love had more to do with beating his business rival than any real enthusiasm for the match.

Glancing at her watch, she frowned. 'Hasn't Suzy turned up yet?' She directed her question at Tina, who had settled into the role of PA and appeared to relish the job.

'Not a squeak from that department. She's always late. Why don't you take her place? You've got similar colouring.'

Lauren hadn't been keen to take part in modelling her own clothes. She had the feeling that those who modelled them had the fantasy of the finished item to wear, whereas she had endured the idea from the drawing-board through every stage of production and had become, in some cases, immune to the charm of the finished garment.

'I'll give her another five minutes. Karen?' She attracted the attention of one of the models. 'Tighten that belt another notch; it isn't supposed to hang.'

The place was awash with perfume, hairspray and fractured egos when Ryan strolled through the mayhem in search of his wife.

'Where is she?' he asked Tina, who was busy sorting out costumes.

'Lauren? She's getting changed. Last screen near the window.'.

'Dishy,' Fi Markham commented, watching Ryan saunter past, hands in pockets. The slight smile on his face showed that he had heard.

'Handsome is as handsome does,' Tina commented. She was very partisan when it came to Lauren.

Lauren looked sideways sharply as Ryan inserted himself behind the screen, pulling her robe around her as he viewed the item of clothing on the hanger.

'Am I to take it you were thinking of modelling that?' he queried indolently, his eyes assessing the filmy dark shadow of a dress.

'Suzy hasn't turned up.' She was abrupt, glancing at her watch. 'I have a schedule, Ryan.'

'It looks transparent,' he commented mildly.

'Not really. It gives the impression——'

'Of the wearer being naked,' he helped her out. 'I don't wish you to appear across leading magazines appearing to be naked. That sort of publicity I don't need.'

Meeting the steely blue gaze, she realised he was forbidding her to wear the dress and she felt her hackles rise.

'Another model would be acceptable, I take it?'

'Certainly. My objection to the dress is that you would be in it. I prefer to keep that beautiful body of yours for private viewing only.'

'My idea of design,' she pointed out, 'is not to make an exhibition of others. I find the outfit perfectly acceptable—— What are you doing?'

'Tina.' He picked up the dress and tossed it to the approaching redhead. 'Find someone else to wear that.'

'You're totally insufferable,' she seethed. 'You enjoy pushing people about, don't you? I suppose you thought it was funny, giving us Richard's office to use as a dressing-room?'

'Richard? Aren't we getting chummy.' His eyes were as cold as ice. 'I see your taste is suspect in more than the matter of clothes.'

She viewed him with disbelief and then laughed. 'You're jealous,' she accused. 'Watch you don't go into overload, Ryan; machines aren't supposed to have emotions.'

'I have emotions, Lauren, some of which, I assure you, you'd prefer I subdued.' Grabbing her lapels, he crushed the silk in his fist as she tried to escape him and brought her back as if she were a rag doll. Her dark hair cascaded loosely around her shoulders, her eyes vivid pools of fury.

'You're making quite an exhibition of yourself,' she reminded him, her heart beating crazily at the expression in his eyes. Something had got under his skin; she had never seen such untempered fury expressed before.

Beyond the screen there was silence and she saw the recognition of the fact grow in his eyes. 'Sometimes with you I don't recognise myself,' he grated, letting her go.

'That must be a relief,' she parried, wishing she hadn't when he hauled her up against him and captured her rebellious mouth in a long kiss that robbed her of breath and will to oppose him. When he let her go, his expression was crushing.

'If you put on that dress, I'll cancel the campaign. It's your decision.' Releasing her, he watched her fall against the wall for support, her mouth the colour of bruised raspberries.

'As you wish.' Lauren wiped the back of her hand over her lips with clearly stated distaste.

Smiling coldly, Ryan departed, walking through a wall of silence that turned into a noisy hubbub as soon as he left the suite of rooms.

Tina rushed to her side, looking concerned, her young face outraged by the paleness of Lauren's skin. Another girl brought her some hot tea, albeit the machine variety.

'Why do you put up with him?' Tina asked naïvely.

Fi Markham gave a groaning chuckle, winking at Lauren.

'Let's get on, shall we?' Lauren pulled together the shreds of her composure, determined not to let Ryan take up any more of her day. The show must go on; wasn't that the old maxim? Ryan didn't want her all over the tabloids in a revealing dress. It wouldn't be the design that created the stir but the fact that she was his wife. It was an understandable point of view, but her opposition was spawned by the increasing tension between them as they played out their roles of man and wife in the Daniels household. Ryan hadn't exploited the fact that he was on home territory and had done just as he had promised, putting their relationship on ice until the mystery behind the robbery was solved. It was the truce that was driving Lauren crazy! Fighting with Ryan was more emotionally satisfying than the civilised façade they affected in front of his parents.

She felt anything but civilised when she discovered just who the 'someone else' was lined up to wear the dress.

Diana Palmer floated into view in the provocative whisper of a dress and left the changing area for the photo-call before Lauren could do more than gasp.

'The agency sent her.' Tina winced at Lauren's frozen expression. 'Do you know her?'

'Would you excuse me a minute?' Lauren stalked to the nearest telephone, punching the number of the modelling agency and waiting impatiently to speak to Melanie Peters.

It appeared Ryan Daniels had cancelled Suzy, expressing the desire for a greater contrast in the girls used, and Diana Palmer had been brought in at the last minute. Putting the receiver back on its cradle, Lauren squared her shoulders.

How she managed to get through the rest of the day, efficiently orchestrating the session, she couldn't recall, but at seven o'clock that night they called it a day and she was left alone in Richard Harrington's office, vaguely acknowledging the cleaners as they came to restore the executive suite.

'Finished?' Ryan leant against the door-jamb, his jacket slung over his shoulder. He looked fresh and clean as usual, only the slight glint of stubble suggesting it was the end of a long day.

Nodding, she picked up her leather holdall, tossing back her hair like a filly sensing danger. It wasn't fair to feel such a *frisson* of excitement in the presence of a man she could very easily hate.

'I'll buy you dinner at Gi-Gi's,' he offered, naming an exclusive wine bar that specialised in French cuisine.

'Are you sure?' She stopped in front of him, anger flaring. 'One of the topics of conversation that I'm sure will come up is why you replaced Suzy without discussion and replaced her——'

'We can talk about whatever you like,' Ryan interrupted grittily, taking her arm and steering her out of Richard Harrington's suite and into the main corridor.

'Why not?' Lauren had reached that particular wooden state where explanations took on the aura of fantasy. 'I don't suppose you'll tell me the truth anyway.'

Ryan pressed the call button for the lift without looking at her. He looked tired, Lauren speculated, wondering bitchily if Diana Palmer was proving a demanding lover. The thought brought with it pain, bone-biting deep.

'Your designs looked good. The typists were enthusing over them, so they've got street appeal,' he told her.

'I suppose you're pleased you might get some return on your investment,' she replied.

Ryan released his breath in an exasperated fashion and waved her into the lift as the doors opened. 'I suppose it's impossible for us to regard the normal civilities?'

'Yes,' she flung back at him, leaning back against the far wall of the cubicle. 'You wouldn't let me model my own design but deliberately put Diana Palmer in it. How do you expect me to feel?'

'I'd like you to trust me but that seems to be expecting too much,' he said.

'Trust you?' Lauren shook her head, her eyes mirroring her incredulity. 'Give me one good reason why I should.'

Ryan regarded her speculatively. 'What are you so worked up about? You needed an extra model and you got one. Why should it matter who it was?'

'Am I to have the privilege of dressing all your lovers?' Lauren was caustic. 'It's humiliating.'

'Don't you like the idea of me sleeping with anyone else?' His eyes held hers, seeing the shock in their emerald depths. 'If you don't, you've got a strange way of trying to keep me.'

'I wouldn't have you gift-wrapped,' Lauren denied hotly, wishing the redness away from her cheeks.

' "The lady doth protest too much..." ' he taunted her softly, Lauren gaining a reprieve from his raking gaze when the lift reached the ground floor and the doors swished open.

The main foyer was empty except for the night-security man who bade them a respectful goodnight. Lauren felt conscious of the contrast they made—Ryan's grey suit, blue shirt and tie blending into a picture of crisp efficiency, whereas she wore designer jeans, a bright yellow T-shirt and a long leather jacket with huge pockets, her hair streaming over her shoulders, managing to look, did she but know it, carelessly chic.

'Will I be all right like this?' She was momentarily side-tracked from the issue of Diana Palmer.

'Yes.' He offered nothing more but his gaze held an element of sexual appreciation that made her toes curl.

Mitch Harrison opened the car door for them and Lauren got in, looking away as Ryan slid in beside her, his thigh brushing hers.

Gi-Gi's was busy, a lively throng that included those coming straight out to dine from the City and more casually dressed diners starting the evening early. It aped the Parisian café and Lauren found herself relaxing into the stylish ambience that imposed no strict rules upon its clients.

'I like it.' She smiled unguardedly to find Ryan watching her and suddenly felt flustered.

He ordered a bottle of claret when the waiter appeared and when he gave her his attention again it was impersonal and she felt her feeling of panic die down.

Lauren decided to have the asparagus and monkfish sauté, and when the waiter returned to fill their glasses with the ruby-red wine he took her order with the addition of *escalope* of salmon for Ryan.

Rolling his glass between his hands, Ryan looked as if he was struggling with something he didn't like much, and then finally he looked up, his brooding gaze capturing Lauren's.

'I owe you an apology.' How much he disliked apologising was clear to see. 'You make me lose my temper, Lauren. I react in ways that are frankly alien to my nature.'

Lauren wondered just how his apology had suddenly made everything her fault. Regarding him in a sceptical fashion, she laughed humourlessly.

'At least you did me the honour of showing some emotion. Maybe there's hope for you yet.'

He considered her criticism. 'You make me sound like some sort of machine. I wish I could close down at night, instead of wondering if you're awake too. You certainly don't look as tired as I feel.' His smile was self-deprecatory and Lauren stiffened her spine, determined not to let this new, more vulnerable Ryan divert her from the Diana Palmer issue.

'I want to know what's going on,' she stated firmly, watching the distant expression take hold again, her frustration evident.

'You will, when I have proof. I'm sure you can appreciate my wish not to make any false allegations...' He smiled at her grunt of disbelief, looking across the bar and lifting his hand in salute to someone he recognised. Lauren turned to see Penny and Derek heading towards their table.

'What a happy coincidence,' she said under her breath, regarding his bland expression. 'You didn't invite them, I suppose?'

'I thought you might want to celebrate.' The charm didn't wash as anything other than surface veneer.

Lauren couldn't believe the audacity of the man. He had known the advent of Diana Palmer into her promotion would bring a demand for some sort of explanation and had plotted accordingly. What better way of avoiding a discussion of the subject than making sure they had company? And he had asked her to trust him!

Greeting Derek and Penny, she had to answer a host of questions about the shoot, telling them she would get the first of the prints the next day.

'Did it all go according to plan?' Penny asked, as interested as her mother in Lauren's launch into the fashion world.

'We had a few minor hitches.' Lauren cast Ryan a glance from between dark lashes. His expression revealed little, a handsomely fashioned mask adept at disguising his meagre stock of emotions. 'One of the models failed to turn up.'

Penny pulled a face of comical horror. 'Oh, you didn't want to model your own things, did you?'

'I didn't have to. Ryan found another model at short notice.' Lauren smiled with mock-gratitude. 'Diana Palmer. Do you know her? She dined at the house the other evening.'

Penny's dark eyebrows drew together in a frown and she directed a questioning glance at Ryan, who merely lifted his glass to his lips and appeared to appreciate the claret.

'Yes. She used to—— She was Richard's girlfriend.'

'Before he set his cap a little higher,' Ryan commented drily. 'I'll call the waiter if you're ready to order.' He cut the conversation dead, leaving Lauren to speculate on what she had learnt. Did Diana Palmer figure as the spoils of victory or had Ryan some other purpose in using the model? Certainly, the very public row they had had over the dress would ensure the matter was high in the gossip ratings.

'What is Ryan up to?' Penny demanded when they took the opportunity to visit the powder-room. 'I know he's got it in for Richard but why parade his ex-girlfriend in front of his nose?'

Lauren shrugged unhappily. 'Maybe he likes blondes. He won't tell me anything.'

Realising Lauren had more to contend with than curiosity, Penny looked sympathetic. 'I'm sure there's nothing like that going on. Why would Ryan marry you if he didn't love you?'

Lauren found the idea of Ryan being in love with her rather remarkable. She began to giggle but there were tears in her eyes and Penny regarded her worriedly.

'I suppose you've fallen for him,' she stated gloomily. 'Derek doesn't think so but the air positively crackles every time you two get close.'

'No one gets close to Ryan.' Lauren took a deep breath, repairing her lipstick, trying to disguise the wounded look that acknowledged her words.

They rejoined the two men and Lauren kept up the pretence of high spirits that drew admiring and laughing glances from those around them. One young man plucked a nosegay from his jacket and kissed the flower before offering the carnation to Lauren.

Ryan's eyes glittered, his hand casually intercepting the flower and throwing it insolently over his shoulder.

'My wife doesn't accept second-hand flowers,' he said.

'Don't knock impulse, Ryan. I know it's beyond your perception but I quite enjoy it,' Lauren retorted.

'Really.' Capturing a welt of her rich dark hair at her nape, he bent his head and kissed her with a brief ferocity of passion that left her reeling. 'There, I've been impulsive twice in one day.'

The other couple didn't know whether to respond to the battle raging between the two or accept the superficial bantering at face value.

'If you want to kiss me, can't you pick somewhere more private, darling?' Lauren asked.

'What happened to impulse?' he murmured, still uncomfortably close, meeting the splinters of glass in her eyes. 'I'll take up your invitation later.'

'What——?' She barely had time to perceive his meaning when the waiter reappeared and she found Derek trying to catch her gaze, no doubt wondering whether he was required to attempt to restore her honour for the second time. The blaze of fire in her eyes convinced her brother that Ryan had his work cut out for him, for her husband, unappreciative or uncaring of the power of the virago at his side, appeared to stoke the flames with provocative gestures of intimacy that left him very much a man on borrowed time.

Mitch Harrison held the door of the Mercedes open, viewing the stiff carriage of his employer's wife with a knowing smile which he quenched hurriedly on meeting Ryan Daniels's gaze. There were going to be fireworks tonight, if he was any judge.

Once they were under way, Lauren opened the intercom to speak to their chauffeur. 'Can you take us back to the studio, Mitch?'

Ryan didn't contradict her despite the slight pause before their driver obeyed her orders. Lauren surveyed him briefly, and the slight arch of his eyebrow mocked her.

'One of your strategic retreats?' she queried, not fooled a bit.

'I was merely admiring your new-found power of discretion,' he replied.

Biting her lip, she quelled an angry retort. She had wanted him on her territory. The Daniels household had too many conventions for her to feel comfortable there. Ryan appeared to share her sentiments, no doubt finding the idea of a slanging match in the home of Sir Charles and Lady Daniels abhorrent.

The studio had changed out of all recognition from the barren warehouse Lauren had taken the lease on. Only the view remained the same, and that twinkled below them, a panorama of purple and gold where the city lights demarcated the river.

The studio celebrated light, bleached stone-coloured walls, pale turquoise carpets, the roof rafters stripped

and varnished with huge three-bladed fans slowly
sweeping in circles. There was a design area, another
with manikins for the finished articles. It was a place of
work but stylish and comfortable as well.

'Quite a transformation.' He idly perused the sim-
plicity of the design. 'You certainly have a flair for this
kind of thing.'

'I didn't bring you here to discuss my interior decorating,' Lauren snapped.

Ryan smiled to himself, pursing his lips thoughtfully,
his survey of the room ending when he came to stand
in front of her.

'Why did you bring me here? I refuse to discuss Diana
Palmer, so if that's what's on your mind forget it,' he
told her.

'It's not just that, is it? Somewhere deep down you
still expect me to be at the bottom of this, don't you?
Do you want me to be guilty? Would it help get your
life back into shape? You don't like things untidy, do
you, Ryan—and I make life untidy for you, don't I?'
she stormed.

'Getting hysterical won't help,' he commented coolly,
watching her fury ignite and catching her wrists as she
launched herself at him. Pushing her hands behind her
back, he laughed at her as she spattered him with insults.

'God, you frustrate me.' She was unable to maintain
the arch of her back necessary to keep her body from
his, and flopped against his chest, unable to sustain the
distance, her hair a dark tangle against his shirt.

'You frustrate me too,' he admitted huskily, his tone
alerting her to the inherent dangers in their proximity.
'Every night when you close your bedroom door.'

Lauren met his silvered gaze as he pushed her hair
back from her heated cheeks with both hands. What she
saw in his eyes made her blood race through her veins.

'How can you want me, when you believe such terrible things about me?' She pleaded for understanding. 'Don't your instincts tell you anything?'

'My instincts confuse me,' he growled, his thumbs brushing against the corners of her mouth. 'My instincts tell me you want me, that you hate the idea of any other woman in my arms. This mouth tells me I have nothing to offer you, that I'm more machine than man. What am I supposed to believe?' His smile was sexy and warm and Lauren found herself in a violent argument with herself. She wanted him! Lord, how she wanted him. And it must have shown in her eyes because his head dipped and took the soft pink vulnerability of her mouth before she had time to think of a protest.

Warmth flooded through her, a spangle of gold dancing through her like sunshine after a storm. Kissing wasn't enough, but a delicious torment to her body's desires. Ryan's hands made their way down her slim curves, moulding the denim of her jeans over her buttocks.

'Do you want me, Lauren?' His lips moved to brush below her lower lip, which quivered with the loss of such heavenly warmth. He nuzzled her jaw and bit softly at the delicate skin under her chin.

'Ryan.' Her voice was a whisper of protest and not very convincing. 'When is this all going to end? I don't think I can stand much more——'

'Soon, I promise.' His warm gaze seemed to be infinitely trustworthy. 'I have to bring pressure to bear on various parties. The methods I use may be a little unorthodox——' He laughed softly at her snort of derision. 'If I went by the book, Lauren, I would never have taken a chance on you.'

Searching his face, her eyes widened at his steady regard, which held elements of an emotion her heart recognised, even if her mind found such a possibility unthinkable.

'Why did you marry me, Ryan? You said you wanted me, then you had to protect me. I'm your wife, I want you to touch me, but we're so far apart, my feelings seem wrong,' she cried.

'What you feel isn't wrong, it's natural. I'm the first man you've slept with, your first boyfriend and lover rolled into one.' He saw the confusion darken her eyes and relented. 'Your emotions are going through a be-lated adolescence. One minute you're raging at me, the next you're melting in my arms. You're turning my life upside-down and the crazy thing is I'm getting addicted.'

Lauren didn't like being compared to an adolescent but gleaned from his words that he found his at-tachment to her as cataclysmic as she did hers to him.

'You're not sleeping with her, are you?' She referred to Diana Palmer, fearing his reply.

'No, Lauren.' Pulling her hips into the hard strength of his, he didn't have to describe his frustration. 'Does this place have a bed yet?'

'I—yes, but I haven't taken the plastic off the mat-tress,' she admitted in a rush, her face pink.

'I can help you with that.' He smiled into her eyes and Lauren melted, finding her mouth shaping itself to his as he succumbed to the temptation of her lips.

There was an unusual domesticity in the task of making the bed with Ryan. When they had slept together before, it had always been done by the staff of whatever establishment they stayed in. She smoothed the cover of the peach-coloured duvet across the bed, which she'd bought in an act of defiance, somewhere to run to if the Daniels household became unbearable.

'Does it go against the grain, sharing the bed with me?' Ryan showed he had guessed something of her thoughts, coming up behind her and wrapping his arms around her middle, kissing her neck and smiling against her skin when she shivered.

'I was thinking about escaping from you when I bought it,' she replied lightly, biting her lip as his fingers plucked her T-shirt from the waistband of her jeans, invading the smooth plane of her stomach with the warmth of his palm. What had happened to all that anger, all that determination to finally set things straight?

Her mouth parted on a soft drag of air as he undid the snap of her jeans.

'Want me to show you what you've been missing?' His voice drugged her senses, his teeth catching the lobe of her ear as his intimate caresses made her head sink back on to his shoulder, depending on his hard frame for support.

Love made her helplessly generous—twisting around in his arms, she pressed her young, ardent body against his, her fingers entwined in the dark gold of his hair, stroking his nape, pushing the blue linen away from his skin when he obligingly pulled at the fastenings for her. She allowed him to strip off her yellow T-shirt, his hands warm on her skin as he undid the front fastening of her lacy bra and lightly coaxed it down her arms.

'You wonder why I don't want the whole world to see you like this?' His eyes moved over her possessively, igniting an answering flame in Lauren.

'It was hardly page-three material,' Lauren demurred, enjoying the hot need in his eyes and the stillness that came over his face when his lean fingers stroked over the soft curve of her breast.

'I've told you, I value my privacy; you're part of that.' The conversation went on despite the growing intimacy between them. Lauren pushed his shirt off his shoulders, following the material down his arms, deliberately exploring the muscles beneath his skin and pressing herself against him in an agony of feeling as he rolled the hard bud of her nipple between his finger and thumb.

Picking her up, Ryan placed her on the bed, bending over her to tug the denim down over her thighs. The abrasive material scuffed her skin and she felt the soothing brush of his fingers over the slight abrasion just above her knee and then the soft touch of his mouth. The slim, tanned thighs with the dark triangle of hair revealed drew the touch of his hands as he reacquainted himself with every inch of her.

'It's a series of firsts with you, Lauren.' Ryan pushed himself up beside her on the bed, kissing her deeply before bending to kiss the rosy tip of her breast. 'You're the first woman who's ever hit me, the first untouched woman to turn into fire in my arms.' He let his smoky gaze return from her body to the lambent flame in her eyes. 'And the first woman I've ever unwrapped a bed with.'

A slow smile curved her mouth, before her eyes darkened, her fingers stealing to his belt to unfasten it. Ryan's fingers traced her arm with light, tickling strokes as she completed the task, taking her hand and pressing it against the male hardness of his desire before she had the chance to free him as he had done her.

'I'm impatient.' He laughed huskily at her protests, before getting rid of his remaining garments and letting his body slide over the softness of hers.

She shared his impatience, her body as starved for his as he was for hers. Ryan surged into her, sensing her need, her whispered words inflaming his blood, her hips fighting with his to set an urgent rhythm that spun them both into a vortex of pleasure that sought to appease ravenous hunger.

Sharing such a deep, primal communion had a compulsive demand of its own. Lauren had previously considered her body a useful vehicle for furthering her fashion ambitions. The appreciation in male eyes had been nothing more than a guarantee of her place in that particular jungle. But Ryan made her glory in her womanhood, made her feel infinitely desirable. She felt special when they made love and couldn't understand how it could be so lacking in emotional content for him.

Her young, slim form arced against the lean, tensile strength of his torso, perspiration glittering on his skin, her tongue darting out to taste the salty liquid, her breath shaking in her throat at the thrusting power of the male, her limbs entangled with his as she harnessed his virile energy and incited him further. He teased her, his movements pausing, leaving them both aching, watching the protest in her eyes grow too far away from words to be spoken. His mouth took hers, hot and demanding as she quivered against him, her hips coaxing the hard angles of his. It was a battle of burning delight, each taking the other to dazzling heights. Lauren's spirit soared and drifted back to earth to grieve over the silence that greeted her love and made her wonder at his arid self-sufficiency.

It took her a while to put it into words. She was relaxed and satiated in his arms and didn't really want to fight again, but curiosity won out.

'Have you never been in love, Ryan?' she asked him, her head pillowed on his chest, her finger smoothing the damp, hair-roughened skin. His heart thundered against her ear, his breathing still erratic from the fervour of their passion.

'Can I have time to consider the question?' He closed his eyes, swallowing thickly. 'Why do you ask?'

She shrugged, watching the track her finger made against the golden hair on his chest. 'I can't imagine you being at the mercy of some woman——'

'Is that how you see love, being at a man's mercy?'

'No—I don't know.' Giving an exasperated groan, she lifted her head. 'How did we end up talking about me?'

'Machines are rather boring in the emotional stakes,' he mocked her, his hands curving over her shoulders. 'You just feed in the appropriate stimulus and they operate.'

'So it seems.' Emerald eyes fringed by dark lashes were wickedly provocative.

Laughing softly, Ryan drew her into the warm strength of his embrace. 'You write one hell of a program,' he murmured against her mouth, silencing any further forays into his past and leaving Lauren none the wiser.

CHAPTER NINE

THE smell of coffee brewing and the blender in operation made Lauren stir into life the next morning. For a moment she was lost, before memory returned and she realised she was in the living quarters of the studio.

A kiss on the tip of her nose made her eyes fly open and she regarded Ryan, who was sprawled beside her, and then frowned as the sounds in the kitchen continued.

'Don't tell me you brought staff?' she asked.

'Mitch,' he informed her, his gaze taking in her tumbled, sleep-flushed state with satisfaction. 'He brought me some fresh clothes.'

'You think of everything,' she breathed, avoiding a kiss and angling her head to look at her bedside clock. It was no use; his mouth began a gentle assault on her neck instead.

'Cancel this morning,' he demanded, 'and stay with me.'

Lauren tried to keep herself covered with the duvet. Yesterday had been filled with heightened emotion, and the fact that she had revealed to Ryan a hunger to match his own made her feel distinctly uncomfortable in the light of day.

'I can't.' She felt terribly hot and wished he'd keep his distance. 'Your marketing team want to select the prints they're going to use. Ryan——!' She squealed as he made an unprintable comment about the marketing team and invaded her space with devastating effect.

Two hours later, when several pots of coffee had been made and consumed by her waiting staff, Lauren emerged from her suite with scarlet cheeks. The navy blue suit she wore, with a short waiter-style jacket and white silk top, were businesslike and feminine at the same time.

'You must have needed your sleep,' Fi Markham, her design assistant, commented slyly, upon Lauren's agitated glance around the room. Silly grins seemed to be plastered over every face.

'Have I had any calls?' Lauren tried to put things back on a formal footing.

'Daniels have rung twice.' Tina didn't quite meet her eyes but brought her a cup of coffee, which she needed.

'Get them on the phone, will you?' she asked.

'No need.' Ryan strolled into the main area, casually fastening his tie. 'I re-scheduled for you.' His eyes danced with amusement, aware of her embarrassment. 'They suggested lunch at one. Don't be late.'

Green eyes sent daggers at his back as he turned away, calling Mitch, who appeared to be quite at home after his sojourn in the kitchen.

Lauren felt the weight of the expectant silence as Ryan and his driver departed. No doubt the more liberated of her team thought she should have instigated divorce proceedings after the public fight they had had the day before.

'I *am* married to the man.' She glared heatedly around the studio. 'Stop behaving as if I've spent a clandestine weekend with the boss.'

'I hope he apologised,' Tina cautioned her. 'He was——'

'What he is or isn't is my business.' Lauren put the record straight, ignoring the 'must have been some night' from Fi Markham. 'Let's get on, shall we?'

Slowly, Lauren gathered together the strands of her composure. It wasn't easy, when every movement of her body reminded her of somewhere Ryan had kissed. Her skin held the memory of the glide and graze of his fingers, a sensual haze clouding her mind and bringing a soft, fulfilled expression to her emerald eyes that stunned her when she caught her reflection.

And what did you learn? she reprimanded herself. Nothing! He told you he wanted you, he showed he wanted you but as for anything else you're as much in the dark as you ever were! All she had discovered was that he wasn't sleeping with Diana Palmer, and even that she had to take on his word.

Passing the security desk at a quarter to one, Lauren was beleaguered by memories of that terrible day when she had been wrongly accused. Would Ryan ever get to the bottom of that particular mystery? Did he really want to? While he had a powerful reason for distrusting her, he could keep her at a safe distance. If he proved her innocence, what had he to gain? If he wished her to remain his wife then it would take more than sexual fulfilment to make her stay. Lauren wanted a full-bodied relationship that included gentler emotions than lust and possession.

'I want him to love me,' she acknowledged aloud to herself as the door closed behind her, the lift cubical empty. 'And,' she added as an afterthought, 'I want him to apologise.'

Meeting with the marketing and the ad team that had secured the Daniels and Blackthorn contract, Lauren was pleased with the quality of the prints and the effects made by her designs. She had her first business lunch, keeping to smoked salmon and salad, her only bad moment viewing the dramatic image created by Diana Palmer in her dress!

'Nice one, that,' Jacko Bryan commented. 'I might use her again.'

Lauren bit back a very bitchy remark. Jealousy, she decided, degraded one's nature.

Ryan appeared in time for coffee. He turned Jacko Bryan out of the chair beside her and flicked nonchalantly through the mounted prints.

'Regret being the other side of the camera,' he murmured, viewing Diana's picture for a fraction longer than he needed to in Lauren's opinion.

She didn't grace him with a reply, his attention captured by an advertising whizz-kid who enthused over the expected impact of the campaign.

Ryan didn't stay long, calling her name and pointing to the door before making to leave the room. She stared at his back, stubbornly staying where she was until he turned and looked around for her, meeting his brusque command with the slight widening of her eyes that pretended interest. 'If you don't mind.' He gestured to the outside corridor with exaggerated courtesy.

'It's nice to be asked.' She smiled sweetly and got to her feet. When they were outside, she made her position quite clear. 'I am not some lackey or dog you're trying to train. Do you always speak to your staff like that?'

'Why do you get so uptight after we've made love? It's supposed to have the opposite effect.'

'What do you want?' she ground out, feeling the soft glow recede rapidly.

'Merely to tell you I'm going to be away tonight on business. I want you to go home, not to the studio, do you understand?'

'I understand English,' she agreed stonily. 'Am I supposed to be in some sort of danger?'

'It's just a precaution. The rest of the family have the same instructions.'

She frowned, her green eyes troubled. 'You are going to call in the police, aren't you, Ryan? If you're dealing with criminals——'

'I know what I'm doing, don't worry.' Tilting her chin up, he placed a warm kiss on her mouth. 'I'll be back for breakfast.'

'Ryan!'

'Enough.' His voice was dismissive. 'I have a healthy sense of self-preservation. I intend to collect on the debt you owe me.' His hand slid inside her jacket to squeeze her breast and Lauren reacted instinctively, merely to have him catch her wrist. 'Breakfast could be really special,' he murmured smokily. 'Keep the bed warm.'

Too incensed to care whether he walked into the very fires of hell, Lauren watched him go in a lather of fury.

It wasn't until she was seated after dinner that evening in the 'daffodil' lounge, the name she had given Lady Daniels's room, that she realised he had manipulated her once again. Ryan didn't like scenes; he circumvented them quite easily. Last night she should have scorched him with her breath; instead, she had succumbed to his sensual skill and proved a very poor opponent.

'Are you worried, my dear?' Elizabeth Daniels surveyed her daughter-in-law with gentle understanding.

Lauren made a brief pretence at non-comprehension. 'Worried? About what?'

Lady Daniels continued with her game of Patience at the small walnut table, a smile playing around her mouth that suggested she was fully cognisant of her son's activities.

'You've been doodling for an hour without drawing anything vaguely constructive. You usually occupy your time more fruitfully,' she observed.

Lauren shrugged, getting up and walking over to the window, her frame tense. 'It's traditional, I suppose, for women to wait while men get on with the action.'

'Frustrating, but in this case wise, I think,' Lady Daniels said.

Lauren couldn't agree. If Ryan had told her more, maybe she would have had more faith in his power to protect himself. Imagining him pitted against a dark, unknown enemy made her fear dreadfully for his safety.

'Ryan went away to boarding-school when he was eight,' his mother reminisced, sounding regretful. 'I worried terribly about him. After his first term, he came back home incredibly changed. At least, it seemed that way to me. He came top of his class, he was in the junior rugby team and seemed to have left me completely behind.'

'I can imagine.' Lauren's tone was dry.

'I don't think you can,' Lady Daniels's voice chided her. 'He wanted to impress his father, you see. He respected Charles.'

Lauren frowned, surprised at her choice of words. Her skin prickled as she sensed her mother-in-law was on the edge of a confession.

'You don't have to——' she began.

'I know, my dear. But I can see that he hurts you with his self-sufficiency. I think you need to understand why he's like that.' She paused. 'Do you love my son, Lauren?'

Emerald eyes met blue and the younger woman's eyes filled with a sad wistfulness that told its own story.

'I thought you did.' The smile welcomed the knowledge. 'It's an unremarkable tale. Charles was as preoccupied with his business as Ryan is. I was spoilt, wilful and restless. I met a man who flattered my vanity and nearly ruined my marriage. Ryan was sent away when the arguments became unbearable. I'm afraid we weren't as discreet as we might have been, and for my sins I lost my son and watched him turn into a polite stranger.' She sighed and Lauren poured her out a measure of brandy, including one for herself. She felt as if they both needed it.

'Charles forgave me,' Elizabeth Daniels revealed. 'But Ryan never did. He viewed marriage as a convenience, to raise a family and make the necessary social contacts. He did...' She paused significantly. 'Until he met you.'

Lauren couldn't share her optimism. 'I don't think he's changed that much.' She viewed the older woman doubtfully as a rich chuckle broke from her lips.

'What did you bring him, except for yourself? He may twist and turn but he can't help coming back. Ryan has never put much effort into maintaining any relationship; it's the first time I've seen him so intensely involved. He loves you, my dear, I'm sure of it.'

Lauren didn't like to disillusion her. He had said she was his queen in this particular game and it was his territory and pride he was protecting; she had merely become part of that.

Sleep deserted her that night. She lay in her bed, wondering what Ryan was up to and where he was. Why didn't he put the whole thing in the hands of the police? Did he still suspect her of being part of the robberies, and had he taken on the mantle of detection himself to protect her?

After an impossible five hours' tortuous ramblings, Lauren got up, showered and dressed. She hated being confined, and watched the early morning light grow in strength with relief.

Bannister brought her tea and some toast, regarding her presence with pained endurance. Lauren wondered

if she'd got him out of bed; he had appeared from nowhere. Probably hung like a bat in the kitchen, she reflected uncharitably.

'There's a telephone call for you, madam,' he informed her as she lifted her second cup of tea to her
lips. 'The caller refuses to give his name.'

A cold trickle of tension ran down her back but curiosity overcame fear and she picked up the extension
receiver.

'Hello, Lauren Daniels here. Who is speaking?'

'Richard.' Harrington's voice was clear and troubled.
'I thought you weren't at the studio. It was just a chance
but I had to check.'

Lauren was none the wiser, her brow creasing in a
frown. 'Why should it concern you where I am, Richard?
It's only six-thirty in the morning.'

'I know.' He sounded disgruntled. 'You've probably
had about as much sleep as I have. How does it feel to
have your husband using your studio to make love to
my girlfriend? He really does like to win on every front,
doesn't he?'

'Your girlfriend?' Lauren was reeling with shock.
'What do you mean?'

'I mean Diana! Who do you think? I'd get rid of
Daniels if I were you. Take him to the cleaners for
alimony; he deserves it.'

The phone went dead and Lauren stared at it as if it
had bitten her. Surely Ryan would never be so deceitful!
How could he take anyone to her studio, when they had
spent the night there together the previous evening? He
let Diana wear your dress, an insidious voice reminded
her. He knew how much that would irritate you. Was
he still paying her back for running away on St Croix?
His ability to hurt and humiliate her far exceeded anything she could do to him.

Collecting her jacket, she marched back down the stairs and out of the house. If Richard Harrington was speaking the truth and not just causing mischief she was going to confront Ryan with his despicable behaviour and hand him back his rings. Bannister called after her but she ignored him. She wasn't in any danger; that was merely a ruse to keep the little woman at home.

Starting up her red Mini, she pressed her electronic key to the automatic doors and pulled out of the grounds of the Daniels mansion; but she had hardly gone any distance at all when she felt the car slow and the engine coughed. A glance at the petrol gauge told her the tank was empty.

It shouldn't be empty, she mused. She opened the car door and looked back towards the house, frowning as she saw petrol streaking the road. Another car pulled up beside her and she was just about to disclaim any need for help when Richard Harrington and another man, who looked vaguely familiar, got out of the car.

'What are you doing...?'

She looked around as Harrington's companion came up behind her, and tried to take flight a second too late. Her arms were grabbed and pinned and something sharp made her flinch as it pressed against her arm.

'It's a terrible thing, jealousy,' Richard Harrington commented whimsically as he held a glass of water to Lauren's parched lips. 'It robs us of reason. Daniels tried to use it to make me do something rash—try a final coup at Daniels and Blackthorn, get caught red-handed with the swag.' He laughed, his blue eyes enjoying the thought. 'He needled me all right but I'm clever enough to think of something a little more appropriate. An eye for an eye.' He smiled at her angry gaze. 'And you do have the most remarkable eyes.'

'Where am I?' Lauren tried to divert his attention, which seemed fixed upon her face. 'Are we at sea?'

'Yes. On our way to Calais. It's quite easy to smuggle a doped woman on to the car ferry. You can imagine the problems at the airport. As long as you're good, you can stay awake now. One squeak and I'll put you back under.'

Lauren couldn't imagine what he meant to achieve, apart from a heavy prison sentence. 'Do you intend to ask for ransom?' She tried to guess his purpose.

'I thought a wife should be worth at least a million— two if he doesn't bargain. Small change to Daniels but I'm not a greedy man.'

'What makes you think he'll pay?' Lauren didn't have Harrington's confidence that she represented any real collateral.

'Oh, he'll pay.' Harrington laughed softly. 'Most men would for you, my sweet.'

Lauren pulled away from the finger that ran around her chin and received a mocking smile. 'And if he doesn't I'm sure we can think of something to recompense me for all my efforts,' he added.

Ryan rubbed his hand over his eyes wearily. 'He hasn't made a move. That doesn't make sense.'

Detective Inspector Cartwright worried his lip with his teeth. 'Maybe he decided to cut his losses. He could have found out we were on to him.'

Ryan's mouth twisted. 'Harrington doesn't strike me as the type to give in easily——' He broke off as the sound of the phone ringing interrupted them.

Mitch Harrison picked up the receiver, listened, his face creasing into lines of consternation. 'It's Bannister. Mrs Daniels left the house about fifteen minutes ago. Her car has been found deserted in the street.'

'Give me the phone.' Ryan pushed himself to his feet, his face tight with tension. Speaking rapidly, he found out about the mysterious phone call. As he put the receiver back on to its cradle, his eyes glittered furiously. Turning to Cartwright, he demanded attention. 'My wife's missing. Her car has been found not far away from my family home. The fuel line was cut. Apparently she had a phone call from a man shortly before she left the house.'

Cartwright frowned. 'You told her——?'

'I explained as much as I could. If it was Harrington calling her, why would she leave the house?' Ryan asked.

'You told her you suspected him?'

'I told her she might be in danger. I couldn't tell Lauren I suspected Harrington; she isn't very good at disguising her feelings.' Some memory made the muscle in his jaw tighten.

Cartwright didn't look very happy about what he was about to say. 'She might have gone with him voluntarily,' he said.

'No!' Ryan denied.

'I have to consider the possibility,' the policeman pointed out doggedly.

Ryan ignored his reasoning. 'Airports.' He snapped his fingers at Mitch. 'Heathrow, Gatwick, private airfields...'

'You think he would leave the country?' Cartwright asked.

'Don't you? Kidnapping is a serious crime and Harrington would know I'd tear this country apart trying to find her,' Ryan said.

'In that case there's the ports as well.'

'I suggest you alert the authorities, Inspector. If anything happens to Lauren, you'll find I have a personal sense of justice.'

The threat was explicit and the inspector wasn't immune to the power of the man he was dealing with.

'Very well, Mr Daniels,' he agreed. 'We'll have their descriptions circulated. Have you got a photograph of your wife handy?'

Ryan opened a drawer in his desk, taking out a folder and spilling a sheaf of photographs over the surface.

'Take your pick,' he said.

Lauren tried desperately to think of a way out of her plight. Sifting through her pocket, her fingers ran over the paste business cards with her name and the studio address on them. Her other pocket had some loose change and a pen.

'I'd like to go to the bathroom.' Her voice was thick, the drug furring her tongue, slowing her up.

'There's no window if you're thinking of escaping.' Harrington took her to the small cubicle. 'I can open it from outside, so don't try and lock yourself in.'

Lauren had no such intention. She was going to write on the back of as many cards as possible and then try and find a way of circulating them.

Fate played into her hands. Brogan, Harrington's accomplice, brought in a tray. She ate, forcing the food down her throat, and slipped the cards beneath the crockery.

'We'll reach Calais in an hour,' Brogan said. 'Hadn't you better put her under?'

'I suppose so.' Harrington was painstaking about drawing up the liquid out of the glass ampoule.

Lauren remained passive, gritting her teeth as he rolled up her sleeve. If she fought and made a noise, there was a good chance they would upset the crockery and her messages would be discovered. This way, Harrington was egotistical enough to allow the steward to collect the tray.

Lauren didn't lose consciousness straight away; she remained in a limbo land where her mind seemed to be floating above her body. No doubt her sheer anxiety was fighting the drug, which had knocked her out physically. Through half-closed eyes she saw Harrington pour himself a glass of wine, his whole manner self-congratulatory.

'What if Daniels won't pay?' Brogan appeared to find Harrington's optimism irritating. 'Diana seemed to think she was on a good thing there. He gave her that modelling job—that made the fur fly. What if he wants rid of this one and just hands the investigation over to the police?'

Harrington laughed. 'Diana was in cloud-cuckoo land. If Daniels wanted to sleep with her, he wouldn't waste time courting her. That isn't his style. He was using Diana to get at me. Daniels has had beautiful women chucking themselves at him since he was out of short trousers—money and class buy that effortlessly. It's Lauren who's different for him. He'll pay all right and, what's even better, he'll suffer agonies wondering what's happening to her. That I'll enjoy.'

Lauren considered his words drowsily. Was she different? A refreshing novelty if so; her lips curled into a lop-sided smile. Were novelties worth paying a million for?

Thuds came from down the corridor. Doors seemed to open and shut, open and shut until they rang in Lauren's drugged brain like a backing track without a melody.

'The steward,' Harrington commented. 'Give him the tray. She's out.'

Brogan looked doubtful but went to the door, shoving the tray at the young man and then closing the door again hastily.

'Try not to look so guilty,' Harrington sniggered.

Brogan snarled an insult at his partner. Lauren vaguely placed him as one of the men who had taken the briefcase from her car. She sensed he was getting impatient with Harrington and wondered if obtaining ransom wasn't quite his cup of tea. Espionage, she thought hazily, was somewhat cleaner than trading in people.

After that things seemed to swim in and out of Lauren's consciousness. The sound of the ferry's engine changed and it appeared to alter direction, no doubt preparing to dock in the French harbour.

There was a strong smell of whiskey coming from somewhere and Lauren shuddered as something splashed her face. Licking her lips, she realised that the whiskey had trickled over her chin and into her hair. She was hauled to her feet and dragged out of the cabin by the two men.

'You shouldn't drink,' Harrington's voice reproached her. 'You know you're not a good traveller.'

Lauren tried to speak but her tongue seemed swollen. She noticed a middle-aged woman look at her with staunch disapproval. The fresh air hit her like a blow and her feet stumbled on the stairs down to the car deck.

A shout made her peer groggily into the distance. Feet pounded the deck and she heard Harrington swear. Then the arms keeping her up pulled away and she fell to her knees as men dressed very much like policemen swarmed on to the deck and ran about like the Keystone Cops.

Someone skidded to a halt beside her and pulled her up. She let her head tilt back to see Ryan looking at her anxiously, his hand framing her face. She felt pathetically glad to see him.

'What's the matter? What's wrong with you? Did you hit your head?' he asked.

'No.' The word barely formed on her lips. Tugging ineffectually at her sleeve, she tried to show him, and with sudden comprehension he pushed up the material and swore at the small mark surrounded by dry blood.

Lauren peered past him as the police dragged Harrington and his accomplice into view. She felt a distant feeling of relief that it was all over, that Harrington had been caught, that the world, at least for her, was safe again.

Ryan turned to see what she was looking at. He appeared to turn in slow motion and launch himself at Harrington, who went down like a nine-pin. It seemed to take a long time before the thin line of blue men moved in to stop Ryan in a very uneven battle. She watched them break and form circles in some meaningless dance and then with a soft sigh slumped to the floor, unconscious.

CHAPTER TEN

RYAN DANIELS joined Derek Walsh at his wife's bed-side, his face immobile; only his eyes hinted at his feelings.

'The doctor says she isn't in any danger. They've done a blood test. Harrington used a high dose of some form of tranquilliser. She should sleep it off within the next few hours.'

'Thank God for that.' Derek was relieved. 'I'm glad that crook's behind bars; maybe we can all have some peace now.'

Ryan nodded, pushing his hands in his pockets and tilting his head to one side, considering the other man.

'No demands for an apology? I'm sure your sister will want one.'

Derek smiled, his pleasant features unblemished by any desire for vengeance. 'Make Lauren happy and I'll forgive you.'

Ryan's hooded eyes were guarded. 'I want her to be happy. I'm not sure I'm the one who can guarantee that for her.' Raking his hand through his hair, he looked for a moment like any harassed male confronted by the mysteries of the female and not knowing what to do about it. 'I'd like to give her some time but if she comes back home with me——' His grimace held an element of humour that made Derek grin.

'You think she should come back to the flat for a while? Resume her old life?'

Ryan nodded briefly, going to stand by the bed and taking Lauren's hand. 'I've got to go and make a statement to the police. I think it would be better if I left it to you to explain. We wouldn't get beyond a row if I suggest it.' Playing with her fingers, he didn't look at Derek Walsh. 'She has a lot of wayward emotions trying to find a home—— If that home's with me, she knows where I am.' Briefly raising her hand to his lips, he placed it back on the coverlet and took a deep, steadying breath before saying goodbye.

Lauren woke up hours later in a hospital bed to see her brother Derek sitting in a chair beside her reading a book. He glanced at her casually and then sat up alert as he saw that her eyes were open.

'I'll get the nurse.' He half rose and rang the bell beside the bed, smiling at her reassuringly. 'You're only in for observation. Just a precaution.'

The nurse arrived and went through the routine observations, smiling with satisfaction. 'You should be able to leave in the morning. Are you thirsty?'

Lauren nodded, the feeling not unlike the hangover she had experienced after her flight from the hotel room on St Croix. Her mind somersaulted, bringing her up to date with the day's happenings in a rush.

'Where's Ryan?' She sat up, her hand lifting to her forehead. 'We were on the ferry and——'

'Ryan's fine.' Derek waited for the nurse to leave. 'He's had to make a statement to the police. They'll want one from you when you feel well enough.' Looking uncomfortable, he tried to find the right approach. 'Ryan seemed to think you would like to come back to the flat for a while. He said you had no reason to feel frightened any more—and that if you needed him you knew where to find him.'

Lauren listened with heavy eyes and then a growing anger. Derek witnessed her expression and found it familiar.

'I think he's right, Lauren. You met in highly emotive circumstances.'

'So we did.' Lauren lay back in the bed, her eyes closing, not wishing to discuss the subject. 'Why don't you go home, Derek, and get some sleep? I'll be all right now.'

'I don't think he wants to let you go, Lauren. He just feels——'

'Does he? I doubt that. Ryan's frightened of feeling. He's going to be perfectly fair and leave the decision up to me. Hell will freeze over before I ask Ryan to take me back!'

Derek Walsh was at a loss to understand how such a reasonable decision on Ryan's part had met with such an explosive reaction. He, too, felt that Lauren needed a breathing space to pick up the threads of her old life and discover whether Ryan Daniels was the love of her life or merely her first encounter with the opposite sex.

Lauren did not return to her old home, feeling that Derek deserved his privacy and that she had grown up a lot since she had lived in the flat. Instead, she moved into the studio. It might not be ideal to live where you worked but at least she was guaranteed to be punctual, she decided flippantly.

Mitch Harrison brought her clothes around, expertly packed. She accepted them wordlessly, pride fuelling a nonchalance she was far from feeling.

'The boss—he isn't going to like it when he knows you've come here. I mean its not like you've got neighbours, is it? Most of the places around here are small businesses,' Mitch said.

'I've got the phone,' she pointed out. 'Anyway, I'm not particularly bothered about "the boss". If he doesn't like it, he can do the other thing.'

Mitch allowed a small grin. 'He's cut up about you moving out but he won't tell you.'

'It was his idea,' Lauren retorted and then looked down into her coffee, wishing she hadn't given, even by the slightest hint, the idea that she was cut up about it too. She brushed a dark wing of hair back from her face. 'I'm sorry, Mitch. If Ryan wants to discuss anything with me, he knows where I am.' She returned his message undiluted.

Mitch sighed but could see she was adamant. 'We'll miss you at the house.' He winked at her. 'You livened the place up a bit.'

'Thank you.' She couldn't help returning his smile. 'I think that's my problem—I make too many waves.'

She spent an hour sorting out her things. Fortunately the bedroom had wall-to-wall wardrobes so she could hang everything up once she had it free of the plastic sheeting. She was arranging her shoes in the rack at the bottom of the unit when she heard the door open, and her spine stiffened as she turned to look towards the open door. Ryan was the only other person, besides two members of her staff, who had a key.

Dressed in a grey suit, with a beautifully blended blue and mauve tie, he looked as if he had just stepped out of Cellophane himself. His hair was combed back from his forehead in sleek gold perfection, his face set in the usual unrevealing mask.

'Does it come to you naturally being awkward or do you work at it?' he enquired, in very unlover-like terms.

'I'm sorry. I don't know what you mean.' She pretended to be innocently baffled.

'I mean, it seems arrantly stupid for a woman who has been burgled, assaulted and kidnapped to want to spend her first night out of hospital alone in a converted warehouse. I doubt you'll get much sleep. I suppose it's some complex artifice to get at me.'

Lauren stood up, dusting her jeans with her hands before putting them on her hips. 'I don't understand any of that. This is my apartment. I've leant on my brother for far too long and I'm starting off the way I mean to go on—alone! I thought you'd be proud of me; you are eager for me to aspire to independence, aren't you?'

'I want you to come back home. But I want you to do that because that's what you want!' Ryan gave her a measured stare, guardedly watching the mixture of emotions expressed in her beautiful emerald eyes.

'I don't remember you asking me what I wanted.' Lauren was momentarily weakened by his admission but the flames of anger were readily stoked. 'You left me in that hospital, sending me a message through my brother, cancelling my membership to the Daniels clan——'

'Lauren——'

'No, you listen for a change. I'll tell you my terms. You have never apologised for accusing me of robbery! You have shown me mistrust and suspicion from the very beginning of our relationship, neither have you ever admitted to loving me.' Her voice became husky despite her attempt to keep it level. 'Well, I want all those things. I want an apology, your trust, and you can open up that vault of a heart of yours and tell me how you feel. Otherwise, you can stay away from me and stop interfering in my life.' She finished with a stubborn lift of her chin, a rebellious glitter in her eyes as she viewed his impassive features.

'I want you to give it six months,' he said calmly as if her demands had never been spoken. 'If you insist on living here then I will have someone watch over the place at night——'

'Six months?' she exploded. 'During which time you'll do what? Take the Chantal Rabannes of this world out to dinner and tell them your wife's on hold?'

'I promise not to give you any reason to be jealous,' he returned in a businesslike tone. 'You can be a little more liberal. I don't mind you dating but if it gets serious then our relationship terminates. Is that clear?'

'And what does serious mean?' she asked scathingly, not believing what she was hearing.

'I mean that I won't condone your having an affair.' Ryan's eyes flashed in anger before he exercised control and the emotion died. 'If you want to go on with our marriage after six months then you can have anything you want in terms of compensation; that includes my heart.' He touched his chest lightly but avoided her gaze.

'It's very much under debate whether you have one.' Lauren shook her head in disbelief. 'I'm afraid I don't agree with your terms, Ryan. I consider our marriage at an end. You can pull the plug on my business if you like but nothing will induce me to wait patiently in the wings for six months while you try to find ways to wriggle out of caring for me.'

Ryan pushed his hands into his pockets, looking as if he'd like to throttle her. 'I would have thought it patently obvious that I care for you. Don't be ridiculous!'

'Well, your way of caring must be pretty mild stuff. The prospect of six months' celibacy is not something I'm wild about!' she asserted.

'Neither am I.' A muscle worked in his jaw and Lauren viewed him speculatively. 'I intend to give you time, Lauren. If our marriage is going to break, I'd rather it happened now than two or three years' time.'

'Good. Consider it over. I will not be dictated to by a cold-blooded machine who thinks he can write safeguards into emotional relationships.'

'I am not a machine.' His voice had a driven note to it but before she could provoke him any further he turned on his heel and went to the door. 'Your business is safe—I promised you backing. Take care of yourself, Lauren...' He paused as if he would say more but decided against it and left without another word.

Lauren gazed after him and then sat down suddenly, feeling drained of energy. She silently called him every name under the sun. In the first burn of anger it was very easy to decide to write Ryan out of her life and concentrate on her designs and re-establishing her social life. Such was the optimism of youth.

A week later, she was missing him badly and would have given everything she owned to be fighting it out with that cool, calculating nature of his even if she did get bruised in the battle.

Elizabeth and Penny Daniels didn't ostracise her from the family, however, and she found herself under fire to do something about their separation. They badgered her into coming back to the family home to attend a promotional function Ryan was hosting.

'I know you have every reason to feel aggrieved,' Lady Daniels admitted, her blue eyes sympathetic as they met Lauren's. 'I can't believe you haven't your own set of terms, my dear; you wouldn't be human if you hadn't. If you're asking Ryan to make himself vulnerable, he won't give in easily.'

Lauren felt a faint blush rise under her mother-in-law's kindly eyes. 'If he cared enough he would,' she said.

'If you cared enough, would you make rules? Stubbornness has a lot to recommend it but it can get in the way at times.'

Lauren didn't know what to do. Ryan had hurt her badly by his autocratic decision that they should spend six months apart. If she gave in and begged to be allowed back into his life, she would conceivably spill her heart to him with no such guarantee that he would do the same. The alternative scenario was that Ryan would still insist on her keeping to his rules and she would be back in the same position with the humiliation of rejection to cope with.

Despite her reservations, she was tempted to see him, even if from a distance. On the night of the Danielses' party she chose her dress, some imp of mischief urging her against merging into the background. She selected a lavender two-piece comprising a long, flowing skirt and a top that had a sweeping neckline and finished just below her breasts, leaving most of her torso bare. Her dark hair tangled around her shoulders, the wild, avenging, passionate sizzle in her veins achieving a pulsating aura that assured her of notice.

Lauren found Ryan easily, her personal radar, where he was concerned, well attuned. He was standing with a group of business associates, attentive but aloof from the situation as if his thoughts were elsewhere. She willed him to look at her and felt a stir of satisfaction when he stiffened in recognition, the cool, masking regard absent. His jaw tightened and, although he didn't move, she could sense his total attention riveted on her.

Luc Rabanne gravitated to her side, his eyes appreciative. 'You look exceptionally beautiful tonight.' He oozed easy charm. 'Chloe tells me you've caused quite a stir in the fashion world. Beauty and talent too—is it surprising Ryan finds you too much of a challenge?'

Lauren's lashes flickered slightly, unwilling to show how the careless comment wounded her.

'I like a challenge. Intelligent women don't frighten me,' Luc added.

Lauren smiled up at him, a flirtatious warmth in her eyes. 'That's interesting.'

Luc Rabanne's appreciation became more overt, his dark eyes heating greedily. Perfectly aware that Ryan was slowly cutting her out of the glittering crowd, Lauren didn't move away as her instincts dictated. Luc was a social hyena, more at home robbing successful men of their wives than achieving anything positive himself. She knew he would give up on her quickly if the game didn't go his way, emotions firmly intact.

'Ah, Ryan.' Luc had a good sense of self-preservation. 'I was just telling your wife how wonderful she looks.'

Ryan viewed the Frenchman with cold hostility. 'Take your act somewhere else, Rabanne. If you had an active brain cell, you'd know when you were being used.'

'So much anger,' the other man mocked. 'Being used can be pleasant. You enjoyed it while it lasted.'

The parting shot made Ryan's hands clench, but Lauren clasped his arm as he made to follow Luc Rabanne.

'He only paid me a few compliments, nothing for you to get irate about.'

Ryan's eyes clashed with hers violently. 'Why are you here? I thought you found this kind of social event tedious.'

'Your mother invited me. I'm sorry, I didn't realise we were supposed to avoid each other. Just pretend I'm not here. We don't have to act married any more, do we?' she pointed out.

'You'll act married when you're around me,' Ryan outlined, his lips barely moving, his grey eyes the colour of slate as he recognised the vengeful gleam enjoying his fury.

'Why should I?' Lauren felt the tension between them tighten a notch. 'You've got your villain, Ryan; you can't threaten me any more.'

'I can promise you something.' He bent his head, speaking in a savage undertone. 'Something that will make prison look like a cosy option.'

'Ryan?' Her fingers pressed against the dark material of his sleeve. 'If you'd just——'

'Just what?' His voice cut into her. 'Give in to juvenile threats like that come-on you gave Rabanne? All that does is prove your immaturity, darling.' The endearment was used as an insult.

'Don't push me too far, Ryan.' Lauren's eyes were the colour of leaves in storm-light, dark and brooding. 'I might just do something we'd both regret.'

'That's your choice.' He chilled her with his gaze. 'But take my advice. Don't play in my back yard. I'm very possessive about my toys. If I can't have them, I'd rather break them than share. We can leave it there, can't we, Lauren?'

The sheer steel in his character bruised her. Oh, yes, she could make him jealous, but it served no purpose. It might have more effect if she had pleaded her loneliness and deep inner craving for him, but then she had her pride too!

A month passed. Lauren worked hard and went out nearly every night. It was an exhausting schedule. Each evening a car would be parked outside the warehouse with Mitch or some other Daniels minion clocking her in and out. At first the car below had given her a feeling of security but then it had hit her like a thunderbolt that Ryan would know her movements, would know whether she returned to her lonely bed or had been tempted elsewhere.

She didn't deliberately set out to throw the cat among the pigeons but when a chance came to be involved in a fashion exhibition in Birmingham she personally resolved to see the organiser and find out details.

When the meeting went on until late she decided to spend the night in a hotel rather than make the return journey. Buying a toothbrush from a chemist's and the necessary nightdress and fresh underwear from a chainstore, she located the hotel. She felt possessed by a restless energy that a boring evening in front of the TV did nothing to abate. Her only consolation was that Ryan wouldn't get his usual report on her movements and that icy brain might be perturbed by the thought that she had more interesting things to do than while away another five months of imposed isolation.

After spending several hours trying to get to sleep, she rose at first light and headed for London. It was nearly seven when she drew up outside the warehouse and wearily unwound her frame from the driving seat. The car had gone, which made her frown. It didn't usually disappear until after eight.

Putting her key into the lock, she let herself in, pondering what she should have for breakfast before seeing Ryan sitting in wait for her and being hit by the sudden realisation that she had done more than perturb him.

'Where the hell have you been?' He pushed himself to his feet, advancing on her with a murderous light in his eyes that made her swallow drily.

'Out. I don't need your permission, do I?' She braved the fury of his gaze, very much aware that he was a strong, muscular male whom it would be wise not to push too far.

'Out where? You haven't been to your brother's; I've checked there—and every other misfit you consort with.'

'My friends are not misfits, they're artistic.' She was momentarily side-tracked. 'And what gives you the right to check up on me? I'm over twenty-one and we're separated!'

'We are not separated!' he roared at her and then seemed forcibly to calm himself, his eyes glittering dangerously. 'Tell me where you've been.'

'You're behaving like a jealous husband,' she pointed out coolly. 'Why should you care? That's part of this experiment, isn't it? To find out whether I can be tempted into adultery——'

'Tell me where you've been before I snap you in half.' Ryan's hands dragged her to him, his fingers biting into her waist as he demanded the truth from her.

'I've spent the night in a hotel room,' she admitted, crying out at the violence of his touch. 'On my own,' she stressed hurriedly, feeling she had probed deeply enough into Ryan's primal emotions; he was in a black rage and would take some calming down as it was.

'You bitch.' He let her go abruptly, pushing a hand through his hair, his anger tempered by exasperation. The haggard expression in his eyes demanded honesty from her. 'This last month you haven't——?'

'Slept with anyone?' Lauren supplied sweetly. 'No. But there's time yet. Another five months is a long time. Would you like me to keep a diary? Then those poor men who sit outside all night could get some sleep.'

'They're here for your protection,' Ryan grated, his eyes brutal in their aggression.

'They're there to check up on me—otherwise you wouldn't be here now!' Lauren slowly let her gaze drift over his body. 'My staff will be arriving in a minute. Isn't there somewhere you should be?'

Her insolence would have provoked a saint. Ryan swept her off her feet and carried her towards the bedroom. Throwing her on to the bed, he pulled off his suede jacket, the T-shirt following revealing the muscular brawn of his chest and shoulders.

'I wouldn't want your diary to be boring.' Ryan advanced on her, cornering her as she tried to scramble off the bed. 'Where are you going, Lauren?' Grabbing a swath of her hair, he pushed her shoulder down back against the bed and slid over her with easy male strength. 'I thought your sort of caring was hot stuff, not well suited to celibacy——'

'Get off me.' Lauren glared at him furiously. 'I don't care if my whole body screams out for you—I'm not going back to that soulless relationship we had before.'

'I haven't touched you yet.' Ryan showed her no mercy, his gaze roaming over her face as if he had forgotten how beautiful she was. 'I think your body might put up more of an argument than you think. Scream away.' His lips grazed her cheek, before his teeth nipped softly at her ear, creating a cold fire that rushed down to her toes and made her shudder. 'Do you have any idea——' Ryan kissed her cheek, his lips rubbing against the stubborn curves of her mouth '—what it feels like to wait all night, wondering if the woman you love has betrayed you or is lying in a gutter somewhere, the victim of some maniac? Fear and rage take turns tearing at your guts——' He watched the realisation of what he'd said take root and her eyes soften. 'And then the manipulating little brat turns up with a glib line in back-chat that would guarantee most people a bed in Casualty and tells me I'm soulless.'

Lauren's heart jumped alarmingly before swelling with joy, her eyes revealing her love for him in return.

'It serves you right.' Her mouth tempted him with soft touches as she spoke. 'You shouldn't have made such impossible conditions.'

'Maybe not.' Pressing his mouth firmly against hers, Ryan kissed her deeply, his fingers undoing the flimsy white jacket she wore and spreading over the silk top beneath, moulding her breast while his tongue stroked slowly against hers in an increasingly sensual message that made her move restlessly, her knee caressing his thigh. His fingers slid over her leg to where the short skirt that matched the jacket rode up, finding the high cut of her flimsy lacy briefs and sliding his hand inside to curve over her buttock.

Lauren revelled in his touch, a feeling of sweet happiness dancing inside her to the heavier rhythm of sexual need. Her mouth clung to his, her slender fingers running through his hair, feeling the heat of his skin as her touch caressed his nape and her palms shaped the strength of his shoulders.

'Undress me,' she whispered, feeling lazy with passion and wanti... to feel his skin burning against hers.

'My pleasure.' Ryan smiled into her eyes, making her heart somersault. He pulled her up into a sitting position and pushed the white jacket off her shoulders, kissing her throat as he did so. The cool air against her back coincided with the slip of silk she wore for a top being drawn up and Ryan's fingers releasing her lacy bra in a swift economy of movement. Throwing the garments aside, he kissed her shoulder and the hollow wells at the base of her throat, his hands stroking her dark mane of hair back over her shoulders. One stray strand hung down, tickling her breast, the rosy tip aching for greater stimulation. Painstakingly, Ryan brushed it way, his touch skimming over the aroused peak, his eyes momentarily riveted on the urgent need expressed in the emerald gaze locked with his.

'Lie back.' His husky tone made her blood beat at a hectic pace.

'I want——'

'I know what you want, darling.' He unfastened her skirt and pushed it down her legs, his mouth closing on her breast with intimate purpose as his hand angled between her thighs. He caressed her, accustomed to the rhythms of her body, inciting her wilfully so that her cries disintegrated from self-conscious gasps into a testimony of need celebrated in low, throaty moans of pleasure that demanded the potency of his possession. Releasing himself from the bonds of clothing, Ryan covered her, feeling the quick rush of excitement he always felt when close to Lauren—his wife.

She reached up for him, her emerald eyes demanding and giving at the same time, her slender frame adjusting to the hard angles of his and inciting his possession. In a fevered haze, Ryan felt his body grow tight against her, instinctively seeking and sinking into the moist heat of her thighs, closing his eyes as he drowned in a magic he'd thought he'd lost for good in the long hours of waiting.

'I'm never going to let you out of my sight again,' he breathed passionately against her throat as Lauren journeyed with him to the edge of wildness and beyond to a country of eternal ecstasy where love ruled supreme.

'You can, you know.' Lauren leant over her husband when he released her and lay back in the bed, his arms above his head in an attitude of total relaxation.

'Can what?' he murmured, eyes indulgent as she stroked the lighter-coloured skin on the underside of his arm.

'Let me out of your sight.' She regarded him with warmth. 'I only do hare-brained things because you drive me to it. If you allow yourself to trust me, I won't give you a moment's worry.'

'Huh.' He laughed low in his throat. 'I wouldn't make promises you can't keep.'

'Ryan,' she reproved, hurt by his scepticism. 'Just now—well, doesn't the way I feel prove anything to you?'

'Yes, I know never to leave you for more than a few weeks on a business trip.'

'You swine.' She hit his shoulder, watching his blue eyes crinkle with laughter. 'I love you—passionately,' she added for good measure. 'And I'm afraid you're going to have to get used to the idea because I will not be put off. Neither will I go back into cold storage for another five months.'

'I think that idea has already come to grief.' Ryan tried to keep his face straight. 'It was for your own good. I didn't give you much choice about becoming my wife— or my lover, come to that.' His fingers stroked along her spine, watching her move her shoulders in cat-like appreciation. 'You hadn't had a very good introduction to the male sex, and I found it extremely difficult——' he tickled her nape and smiled at her blissful expression '—to be as patient with you as I promised myself I would be.'

'I don't remember you being patient at all.' She kissed his chin, a knowing glint of laughter in her eyes.

'I wanted you before you got caught with your hand in the till,' he informed her, emitting a swift exclamation of pain as she bit his ear.

'I was totally innocent,' she insisted.

'On all counts,' he agreed, watching her warily. 'Which is why I thought you should have your taste of freedom before you decided to settle down with me. I know all hell will let loose if you try to leave me again.'

'I won't,' she pledged solemnly. 'Your mother thinks you were badly affected by the problems in her marriage. She still grieves for the part of you she lost.'

Ryan frowned, looking a little uncomfortable with her open scrutiny. 'I do love my mother but I suppose I always came back from school thinking she might be gone. I've forgiven her; she's only human, I realise that now. You can't turn back the clock, Lauren; I'm not a little boy any longer.'

'No,' she agreed, a secretive smile playing about her mouth that he had no trouble deciphering. 'You could let her know she's still important to you, though; sometimes we women need reassuring.'

'I need reassuring too.' He put a hand behind her neck and brought her mouth down to his, kissing her in a languid manner, turning her underneath him when the mood changed into something more vibrant.

'Tell me something,' he asked casually, his eyes holding hers. 'What made you go with Harrington? Penny and Derek had already made him one of their suspects; you must have been suspicious.'

Lauren groaned; she had forgotten about that. 'I'd rather not talk about it,' she said faintly, burying her face into his shoulder.

'Don't you think we should lay all our ghosts?' Ryan pursued her relentlessly. 'It's been going round and round in my mind. How could Harrington make you leave the house? I couldn't believe you actually liked the worm——'

'No,' she agreed hastily. 'It was nothing like that.'

'Tell me.' He was determined.

She did. Watching his face change, she hurried over her confession, realising her little homily on trust could well be considered on her own part.

'You thought I would take Diana Palmer to your studio, your bed, and make love to her? I'd already told you there was nothing between us,' he said.

'I know—but you let her wear the dress and I didn't know you were trying to provoke Harrington. If you had let me into your confidence, Harrington wouldn't have been able to hoodwink me.'

'You'd have come up with some other damn fool scheme,' he muttered ungraciously. 'Like searching my cabin for evidence.'

'That wasn't my idea,' she protested hotly. 'I was trying to keep Derek out of trouble.'

'Yes, I know,' he relented, framing her face with his hands. 'You have every reason to hate me. If it's any consolation, I wanted to believe you had nothing to do with the security leaks; I was just too much of a coward to admit my real reasons for keeping you with me.'

'Which were?' she teased gently.

'Besides keeping you out of trouble, my motives were purely selfish. I'd never met a woman I wanted so badly. After you refused my dinner date, that first time we spoke, I felt a grim satisfaction when you fell neatly into my hands. When you told me about the time you were fostered, it made me feel ashamed. I swore I'd never force you into anything you couldn't handle——' Shaking his head, he gave her a deep, meaningful look. 'You gave me some bad moments. That night you stormed into my study, I nearly followed you out on my knees.'

She laughed, remembering her own frustration. 'You were so pigheaded, refusing to tell me about Diana Palmer. I was crazy with jealousy.'

'I know how it feels,' he admitted roughly. 'This has been the longest month of my life.' Bending to kiss her, he paused as noises came from outside. 'It sounds as if your team are back.' He jerked his head toward the door where sounds of people arriving came through to them.

'Suddenly, I find work rather unappealing,' Lauren admitted, an imp of mischief shining in her eyes.

'We could try a joint venture,' he suggested huskily, smiling as he felt her hands sliding wickedly over his body.

'I think that's a very good idea,' she laughed softly as Ryan showed her he thought so too.

Accept 4 FREE Romances and 2 FREE gifts

Mills & Boon

FROM READER SERVICE

An irresistible invitation from Mills & Boon Reader Service. Please accept our offer of 4 free Romances, a CUDDLY TEDDY and a special MYSTERY GIFT... Then, if you choose, go on to enjoy 6 captivating Romances every month for just £1.70 each, postage and packing free. Plus our FREE Newsletter with author news, competitions and much more.

Send the coupon below to: Reader Service, FREEPOST, PO Box 236, Croydon, Surrey CR9 9EL.

NO STAMP REQUIRED

Yes! Please rush me 4 Free Romances and 2 free gifts!
Please also reserve me a Reader Service Subscription. If I decide to subscribe I can look forward to receiving 6 brand new Romances each month for just £10.20, post and packing free.

If I choose not to subscribe I shall write to you within 10 days - I can keep the books and gifts whatever I decide. I may cancel or suspend my subscription at any time. I am over 18 years of age.

Ms/Mrs/Miss/Mr _____ EP30R

Address _____

_____

Postcode _____ Signature _____

Next Month's Romances

Each month you can choose from a wide variety of romance with Mills & Boon. Below are the new titles to look out for next month, why not ask either Mills & Boon Reader Service or your Newsagent to reserve you a copy of the titles you want to buy — just tick the titles you would like and either post to Reader Service or take it to any Newsagent and ask them to order your books.

Please save me the following titles:		Please tick	√
HIGH RISK	Emma Darcy		
PAGAN SURRENDER	Robyn Donald		
YESTERDAY'S ECHOES	Penny Jordan		
PASSIONATE CAPTIVITY	Patricia Wilson		
LOVE OF MY HEART	Emma Richmond		
RELATIVE VALUES	Jessica Steele		
TRAIL OF LOVE	Amanda Browning		
THE SPANISH CONNECTION	Kay Thorpe		
SOMETHING MISSING	Kate Walker		
SOUTHERN PASSIONS	Sara Wood		
FORGIVE AND FORGET	Elizabeth Barnes		
YESTERDAY'S DREAMS	Margaret Mayo		
STORM OF PASSION	Jenny Cartwright		
MIDNIGHT STRANGER	Jessica Marchant		
WILDER'S WILDERNESS	Miriam Macgregor		
ONLY TWO CAN SHARE	Annabel Murray		

If you would like to order these books in addition to your regular subscription from Mills & Boon Reader Service please send £1.80 per title to: Mills & Boon Reader Service, Freepost, P.O. Box 236, Croydon, Surrey, CR9 9EL, quote your Subscriber No:.................................... (If applicable) and complete the name and address details below. Alternatively, these books are available from many local Newsagents including W.H.Smith, J.Menzies, Martins and other paperback stockists from 14th May 1993.

Name:...

Address:..

....Post Code:.........................

To Retailer: If you would like to stock M&B books please contact your regular book/magazine wholesaler for details.

You may be mailed with offers from other reputable companies as a result of this application. If you would rather not take advantage of these opportunities please tick box ☐